PUFFIN BOOKS

THE SEARCH FOR THE GOLDEN PUFFIN

In 1941, Merlin the magician saves a young man from a terrible fate. In return for his life, the young man has to promise to find the legendary Golden Puffin given to King Arthur by Merlin hundreds of years before. But his quest cannot begin for fifty years and by that time the young man is a grandfather!

When Anna and Ryan find Grandpa inventing a time-machine in his garden shed on New Year's Day 1991, they think he's crazy! But soon all three of them are off on the quest to find the Golden Puffin. To do this, they have to travel fifty years through time, stopping at each year to solve a puzzle set by Merlin. Each puzzle they solve correctly gives them a clue which will help them to find the Golden Puffin.

Now YOU can join Anna, Ryan and Grandpa and travel through time in your armchair time-machine. YOU can solve the puzzles and find out some amazing facts about the last fifty years at the same time. YOU will also have the chance of a lifetime to win an exact replica of the Golden Puffin itself.

Part story, part game, set in the real world of the last fifty years – 1941 to 1991 – fifty glorious Puffin years!

THE SEARCH FOR THE
GOLDEN PUFFIN

ILLUSTRATED BY STUART TROTTER

PUFFIN BOOKS

PUFFIN BOOKS

Published by the Penguin Group
Penguin Books Ltd, 27 Wrights Lane, London W8 5TZ, England
Viking Penguin, a division of Penguin Books USA Inc.
375 Hudson Street, New York, New York 10014, USA
Penguin Books Australia Ltd, Ringwood, Victoria, Australia
Penguin Books Canada Ltd, 2801 John Street, Markham, Ontario, Canada L3R 1B4
Penguin Books (NZ) Ltd, 182–190 Wairau Road, Auckland 10, New Zealand

Penguin Books Ltd, Registered Offices: Harmondsworth, Middlesex, England

First published 1991
1 3 5 7 9 10 8 6 4 2

Text copyright © Complete Editions, 1991
Illustrations copyright © Stuart Trotter, 1991
All rights reserved

Printed in England by Clays Ltd, St Ives plc

CONTENTS

INTRODUCTION

The Search for the Golden Puffin **takes you on an exciting adventure through fifty years in time, where you will help to find the legendary Golden Puffin.**

Begin by reading the story and meeting Grandpa, Anna and Ryan. You'll find out about the history of the Golden Puffin and how Merlin saved it from destruction and hid it in a safe place. It's your task to discover where he hid it, and if you can do this, you have a chance of winning a golden puffin.

To do this, you have to solve fifty puzzles that cover a period of fifty years. The first puzzle is set in 1941 and the last one in 1991. Each puzzle has a box like this at the bottom, offering three (or sometimes only two) answers.

If you choose . . .	Secret Message letter	Next go to . . .
1	C	1971
2	M	1958
3	L	1969

If you think the correct answer to the puzzle is 1, your Secret Message letter is C. Turn to the back of the book and in the 1941 box write the letter C. Then turn to the 1971 puzzle and have a go at solving that. Keep going until you reach 1991. The puzzles will take you forwards and backwards in time in a special sequence designed by Merlin.

Merlin's Secret Message
Merlin's Secret Message will help you to solve the final clue and find the Golden Puffin. Every time you answer a puzzle, you'll get a letter to enter in the Secret Message. If you choose the correct answer, you will get a correct letter in the message. If you get a puzzle wrong, or *very* wrong, you'll get a wrong letter. So when you get to the end of the book and read the message, the more correct answers you chose, the more sense the message will make. Try to get as many correct answers as possible – that way you'll find the last question easy.

When you get an answer wrong
Every puzzle offers you a choice of three answers (sometimes only two). One of these answers is correct. Another is nearly correct. And the third is totally wrong – the worst choice you can make. Your choice of answer influences the letter you get in your Secret Message. It also influences which puzzle you go to next. If you choose the correct answer, you'll go to the next puzzle in the time-sequence. If you choose the 'nearly correct' answer, you'll miss one year in the time-sequence. And if you choose the totally wrong answer, you'll miss two years in the time-sequence. This means that if you get all the answers correct, you'll do fifty puzzles and have a correct Secret Message. If you get some puzzles a bit wrong, you'll miss a year here and there and have some gaps in the Secret Message. And if you get some puzzles *totally* wrong, you'll miss more years and have more gaps in the Secret Message. So the more careful you are and the more answers you get right, the easier it will be to find the Golden Puffin.

THE SEARCH FOR THE
GOLDEN PUFFIN
THE STORY

'Ouch!' came a cry from the shed.

'Grandpa, what are you doing in *here*?' asked Anna, opening the door. 'Grandma says you're supposed to be laying the table – it is New Year's Day and you know she always cooks something special. She's very cross with you.'

'Then you'd better come in quickly, before she finds out where I am,' hissed Grandpa, sucking his thumb which he'd hit with a hammer. He stuck his head out of the door, to check that Grandma wasn't about, and then shut it firmly.

'Are you making another invention?' asked Ryan, pointing to what looked like Grandma and Grandpa's old flowery armchair in the middle of the shed. Except that it wasn't *quite* like their old armchair, because *their* chair hadn't had wires coming out of the back of it, or an old hairdrier-hood sticking up from the top. Or a steering-wheel, or skis. Or an electronic control panel with a solar-powered battery-pack.

'Yes, what is this?' asked Anna.

'Hmmm,' said Grandpa, looking shifty. 'That? Oh, that's nothing at all. Maybe we'd better go in for lunch.'

Anna didn't believe a word of it. 'It doesn't look like nothing to me,' she said sternly, and she sat in the armchair and bounced up and down.

'What happens if I press these?' She tapped a few keys on the control panel.

'Don't do that, please,' said Grandpa, looking annoyed.

Anna inspected the big red dial on the left arm of the chair. It was pointing to the number 1941, and on top of it was a shiny green button.

'If this is nothing, Grandpa, it won't matter if I press it, will it?' she said naughtily. And before Grandpa could stop her, there was a shower of sparks and a loud humming noise and the shed began to vibrate. Ryan watched as the armchair and Anna in it began to fade slowly away – and then Grandpa leapt over and pulled all the wires out of the battery.

He grabbed a blue handle on the right-hand arm of the chair and gave it a tug, and everything stopped fading and grew quiet again. A cloud of blue smoke hung in the air. 'Phew!' sighed Grandpa, and he mopped his forehead with an oily rag. 'That might have been extremely serious.'

Anna scrambled out of the chair, looking quite pale. 'What happened?' she said. 'Everything went misty. It was as if I was going to disappear.'

'Mmmmm,' said Grandpa, picking up his spanners and reconnecting some of the wires he had pulled out.

'What *is* it, Grandpa?' Anna asked. 'Is it a flying hairdrier? Or an automatic ski-chair?'

'Not exactly,' muttered Grandpa.

Ryan looked at the dial turned to 1941, and then at the other numbers round the rim. 'If you ask me,' he said quietly, 'I'd say it was a time-machine.'

'Would you now?' said Grandpa, looking up. 'Well, in that case, Ryan my lad, you'd be just about right.' But before anyone could say another word, they heard footsteps outside the shed.

'Are you in there, Arnold?' called Grandma. 'Anna, Ryan, it's lunchtime!'

● ● ●

'It was like this,' explained Grandpa, when they'd had their lunch and done the washing-up and were safely back in the shed. 'In 1941 I got my first job. It was in the post-room of a company called Puffin Books – they published books just for children. The company got its name from a beautiful little puffin made of pure gold, with sapphires for its eyes. The puffin was said to be very old. Some people even thought that it had magical powers. They said it had been given to King Arthur by Merlin the magician, to remind Arthur of the puffins that lived on the cliffs around his home in Cornwall. They said that Merlin would always protect the puffin and never allow it to be destroyed – because if it was destroyed, then England would be destroyed by dark forces too.'

'Wow!' said Anna and Ryan together.

'Did you believe all this?' Ryan asked, thinking that it all sounded a bit far-fetched. 'You know, Merlin and dark forces and all that stuff.'

'No, of course not,' said Grandpa dismissively. 'All I knew was that there was this little golden puffin in a glass case in the office, and that sometimes its eyes seemed to be following you around the room. But that didn't bother me. And then one day something strange happened.'

'What?' cried Anna.

'If you'd give me a minute, I'd tell you,' snapped Grandpa. 'I was working late at the office. I'd stuck all the wrong labels on the packages of books and I had to stay behind when everyone else had gone to sort them out. It was late and outside everything was pitch black, because the war was on, you know, and no one was allowed to show any lights, in case bombers came flying over London and dropped bombs. Anyway, it was all misty and nasty out and I was working away in the packing-room, when I heard something. A mysterious noise coming from the office where the Golden Puffin was kept in its glass case. So I crept up the stairs and looked into the room to see what was happening.'

'What was it?' asked Ryan. 'Burglars?'

Grandpa shook his head. 'It was an old man. He was tall and wearing a big black cloak that swirled around him. And the room was glowing – a sort of greenish glow.'

'*Spooky*,' whispered Ryan.

'*Very* spooky,' agreed Grandpa. 'He had long fingers with gold rings and a tall stick with a strange symbol on the top. I hid behind the door and watched as he lifted the glass case and picked up the puffin. Then he hid it in his cloak.'

'Ooooooooooooh,' said Anna. 'What did you do?'

'I sneezed,' said Grandpa.

'Oh-oh,' said Ryan.

'Exactly,' nodded Grandpa. 'He heard me and held out one hand with its long fingers with their long nails, and he beckoned. And the door began to swing open – *all on its own*. I was left with nowhere to hide.

'"Come here," said the old man, and my feet began to move all by themselves. Before I knew what was happening, I was standing right in front of him.

'"Young man," he said, and I couldn't keep my eyes off him, because he looked so strange – sort of cruel, but kind at the same time. "Young man, you are in great danger. The Golden Puffin is now safe with me. But you . . ." He shook his head as if he knew something I didn't. Then he said, "I have decided, young man, that I am going to break the rules of time and destiny to keep you safe. To repay me for this favour, it will be your job to seek out the Golden Puffin from where I have hidden it and restore it to its rightful place. Your quest will not begin for fifty years. Then, if you can unravel my puzzles, you may find it again."'

Grandpa paused, remembering all he had seen and heard that night.

'What happened after that?' asked Anna.

'After that,' Grandpa said, 'he disappeared in a puff of green smoke.'

14

'That only happens in fairy-tales!' protested Ryan.

'It's as true as I'm sitting here with you now,' insisted Grandpa. 'There was a flash and he was gone. And the puffin with him. And the next thing I knew, there was another huge crash and the ceiling fell down on top of me.'

'He knocked down the building?' gasped Anna.

'Not *him* – a bomb!' cried Grandpa. 'It was 1941, the war. Bombs dropping all over Europe – and one right on top of me! They had to dig me out of the rubble.'

'But weren't you hurt?' Anna asked.

Grandpa laughed. 'Not a scratch! That was the danger he'd been talking about, I reckon. The bomb would have destroyed me and the puffin.'

'And let dark forces take over England,' added Ryan.

'Exactly,' nodded Grandpa. 'Me and that puffin would've been flattened like pancakes in the normal course of things. But he was true to his word, that chap. He kept me safe. And now it's 1991, fifty years on, and it's my job to find that puffin.'

'You don't think it might all have been a dream, do you?' Anna suggested.

'Many's the time I've told myself that it was just a dream,' agreed Grandpa. 'But it wasn't, and there are two things that prove it.'

'What are they?' Ryan wanted to know.

'First, though they sifted the rubble of that building as

carefully as your grandma sifts flour when she's making Yorkshire puddings, they never found so much as a feather of that golden puffin. Not even one of its sapphire eyes. And secondly . . .' Grandpa reached into his pocket and pulled out a scrap of parchment, '. . . I found this under my pillow this morning.'

He unrolled it for them to see. It was brown and crinkly, but the writing was clear enough. In curly black letters Anna and Ryan read:

> In a Cornish river find a beast of burden,
> Then add loads or plenty to find an ancient kingdom,
> Where in modern England this ruined castle lies,
> There, if you look for it, you will find the prize.
> To start you on the quest, go back to forty-one
> And follow Merlin's trail until the journey's done.

'What does it all mean?' asked Anna.

'I don't know,' said Grandpa. 'You'd have to be Mastermind to work it out.'

'So what are you going to do?' asked Ryan.

'I'm going to do the only bit I can understand,' laughed Grandpa. 'Go back to forty-one . . .'

'*Nineteen* forty-one!' cried Anna. 'You have to go back fifty years – so you've built a time-machine!'

'Precisely,' said Grandpa, pretending to be cross. 'I was just making final preparations to set off into the past, when you two came and interrupted me. I'd planned to be gone before lunch – and now, I suppose, you'll want to be coming with me.'

'Yes!' they both yelled.

Grandpa thought about it for what seemed ages. 'It could be dangerous,' he said at last. 'On the other hand, that Merlin chap seems to know what he's doing. He kept me safe from the bomb, after all. And if I leave you here, you'll only go and tell Grandma what I've been up to, and when I get back – *if* I get back – there'll be hell to pay . . .'

'You never know,' added Ryan, 'perhaps we'll be useful. Three heads might be better than just one.'

'Yes,' agreed Anna. 'You can't go on your own – we'd worry about you.'

Grandpa thought some more. 'All right,' he said at last, 'but if there's any sign of danger, you're coming straight back here. Do you understand?' Anna and Ryan nodded. 'Well, if that's straight, we may as well be on our way.'

Grandpa sat in the armchair and the children squeezed in on each side of him. He checked the red dial, released the blue handle, pressed a few keys on the control panel and suddenly the chair vibrated into life. Sparks popped from the hairdrier and smoke began to swirl from beneath the feather cushions. Ryan's thumb was poised over the green button.

'Now?' he asked Grandpa.

'Now,' nodded Grandpa.

The shed was filled with a loud humming sound, and after a few seconds the armchair and its three occupants seemed to fade out of focus. And a minute later, when Grandma opened the door to see if they'd like some tea and cakes, the shed was quite empty.

'Here you are at last!' boomed a voice. 'You took your time.' The three time-travellers stared all round, their eyes adjusting to the gloom. 'And you've brought *chil-dren*,' said the voice disapprovingly. 'I didn't tell you to do that.'

Grandpa turned to face the tall, dark figure standing in the corner of the room. Anna and Ryan were aware of a pair of piercing green eyes watching them intently.

'We wanted to come and help,' Anna said bravely. 'And to make sure Grandpa was all right. He's getting on a bit, you know. His rheumatism's bad.'

Merlin smiled. 'Is it really? The last time I saw him he was just a lad. And to think he now has grandchildren and rheumatism too!'

Grandpa looked embarrassed. 'The thing is, Merlin, is this quest of yours going to be dangerous? Only I don't want Anna and Ryan getting hurt.'

Merlin shook his head. 'No, it's not very dangerous. They might even find it fun. And they could come in useful, I suppose. We'll let them stay.'

'Thank you very much,' said Ryan, looking around at the old-fashioned offices. 'Have we really come back in time to 1941?'

'You certainly have,' Merlin said. 'And I have just a few minutes to give you your instructions.'

'Fire away,' said Grandpa. Anna and Ryan listened hard.

'Your quest is to find the Golden Puffin, which I have hidden in a safe place,' Merlin explained. 'To find it, you have to travel fifty years through time, stopping at each year and solving a challenge before you can journey on to the next. If you solve enough mysteries and puzzles, you'll eventually get back to 1991 – and with a bit of luck, you'll be able to work out where the Golden Puffin is kept.'

'It doesn't sound too hard,' said Anna.

'And we've got the armchair, so travelling through time won't be too difficult,' added Ryan, patting the feather cushions.

Merlin looked at Grandpa's time-machine questioningly. 'Your time transport doesn't look very reliable to me,' he commented. 'Leave your travel arrangements to me. I can transport you quick as a flash – or quicker.'

'All right,' said Grandpa.

'And one other thing,' remembered Merlin, 'you're not, whatever you do, to tamper with time.'

'We promise not to,' said Ryan.

Merlin swirled his cloak around him. 'In that case, it's time to start the search. Good luck!'

1941

'Your first challenge,' said Merlin, 'is to get out of here as quickly as you can, because this building is about to be flattened by a bomb! You need to get to the safety of St Paul's Cathedral.' He waved his long fingers and a

The First Challenge
Check the three routes on the map. Whose directions will get them safely to St Paul's?

If you choose . . .	Secret Message letter	Next go to . . .
Grandpa's route	P	1981
Anna's route	L	1948
Ryan's route	Y	1959

huge map seemed to appear from nowhere. 'Here's a map that will help you choose your route,' said Merlin. 'Goodbye!' And with a puff of smoke, he disappeared.

'Look,' said Grandpa, 'some of these roads have been blocked by fires and dangerous buildings and unexploded bombs. I know, we'll go over Westminster Bridge, take the first left, then left again. That should get us to safety.'

'Oh no it won't,' said Anna. 'I think we should stay on this side of the river and cross Waterloo Bridge, then turn right.'

'Well, I think we should go up to Trafalgar Square and turn right, that'll take us straight to St Paul's,' said Ryan.

Events of the year

Britain at war with Germany. London air raids – 100,000 bombs dropped in a single day.

In December, America joins the war after Japan bombs their ships at Pearl Harbor.

The last execution at the Tower of London takes place: German Josef Jakobs is shot for spying.

1942

'Where are we now?' asked Ryan, jumping out of the way just before he was run over by a porter trundling a trolley. 'I think we must be invisible!'

'I wouldn't be surprised,' said Grandpa. 'And as for where we are, it looks very much like King's Cross Station to me.'

'But what's going on?' Anna wanted to know.

'Evacuation, that's what,' explained Grandpa. 'You see all these children with suitcases and gas masks and labels? They're going off to live in the countryside, where they're safe from the bombs.'

Anna and Ryan looked around. They were glad that *they* weren't being evacuated. 'But what about the next challenge?' asked Ryan.

'It's here!' called Anna, who'd been looking at the posters. 'Look!'

Events of the year

Britain and allies at war with Germany, Japan and Italy.

In England, sweets are rationed for the first time.

The King, George VI, has lines painted round bathtubs at Buckingham Palace, so that no one uses too much water.

KING'S CROSS CHALLENGE.

On the bench to your left, are Sidney, Cyril, Sarah, Simon and Susan, pupils of the Dame Augusta Thwackhem School, who are being evacuated to Scunthorpe. As you can see Sidney, Cyril, Sarah and Simon have numbered labels round their necks. What number should Susan be?

If you choose . . .	Secret Message letter	Next go to . . .
10	E	1967
13	C	1989
18	O	1973

1943

Grandpa, Anna and Ryan found themselves in a gloomy street. 'This is creepy,' said Ryan, as he spotted a figure lurking in the shadows. 'There are some strange people hanging around. Do you think they could be spies?'

'They might be,' said Grandpa. 'During the war, we were all warned not to talk to strangers or tell anyone secrets about our work. There's nothing the Germans would have liked more than to know our secret plans.'

Anna tugged at Grandpa's sleeve. 'Look over here, both of you.' She pointed to a piece of paper that had been stuck on to a lamp-post. Grandpa took it down and this is what they read:

Spycatcher Challenge

One of the people in this street is a spy, who has just stolen some top-secret information. Using these clues, can you catch the spy?

- *The spy is walking west*
- *The spy is wearing a navy-blue hat*
- *The spy doesn't have a pet*
- *The spy doesn't eat sweets*
- *The spy hasn't read yesterday's paper*

Events of the year

Special 'bouncing' bombs are dropped by the Royal Air Force to destroy a dam on the German River Ruhr. 617 Squadron, who drop the bombs, become known as the Dambusters.

School uniforms in any colour other than blue or grey are banned.

Because of a shortage of turkeys, nine out of ten families have to go without one this Christmas.

If you choose . . .	Secret Message letter	Next go to . . .
(wrong answer)	R	1970
(correct answer)	U	1987
(very wrong answer)	P	1958

1944

'Well I never,' muttered Grandpa, and he took off his glasses and polished them on his jumper. 'What a surprise – and an honour too.'

'Well you never what?' Anna demanded, looking around the room they'd arrived in. 'Who is *that* man?' She pointed towards the mirror, where an elderly gentleman was tying his bow-tie.

'That,' said Grandpa proudly, 'is Mr Churchill – or Sir Winston, as he became known. He was the Prime Minister who led Britain through the war. And look, he's wearing his special siren suit.'

'I thought it was just a boiler suit,' said Ryan.

Anna was getting impatient. 'What are we supposed to do here?' she asked.

Just then Ryan spotted a party invitation, with a gold crown at the top of it, which was lying on a table. 'I know where he's going – and I think I've found the next challenge.'

Events of the year

6 June – D-Day. British and allied troops invade Europe, landing in northern France. By August they reach Paris.

The school-leaving age is raised to fifteen.

Streetlights and lights in buses and trains are switched on for the first time in five years.

The Churchill Challenge

As you can see, Mr Churchill is checking his tie before going off to dinner at Buckingham Palace. Which of these pictures shows his reflection as he sees it in the mirror?

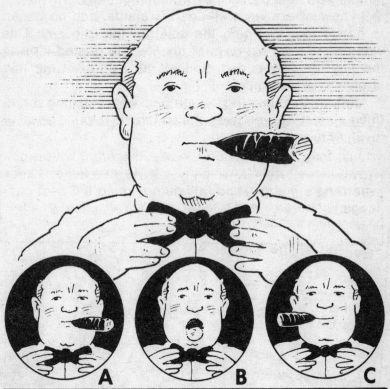

If you choose . . .	Secret Message letter	Next go to . . .
A	C	1977
B	M	1960
C	T	1986

1945

All of a sudden, the three time-travellers found themselves surrounded by huge crowds of singing and dancing people. They were waving flags and having a wonderful time, and a lot of them were dressed in military uniforms. Anna and Ryan grabbed Grandpa's jumper and held on, so they wouldn't get lost.

'I know where we are!' cried Grandpa, and *he* began to dance too, swinging the children into the air. 'This was one of the best days of my life,' he panted. 'It was the day the war ended, and we all came out into the streets to celebrate.'

Anna wasn't listening though. She was watching something else. 'Hey, you two,' she called, 'I've found another mystery to solve . . .'

The Mystery of the Missing Cake
Study the words and pictures carefully and then decide who stole the victory cake!

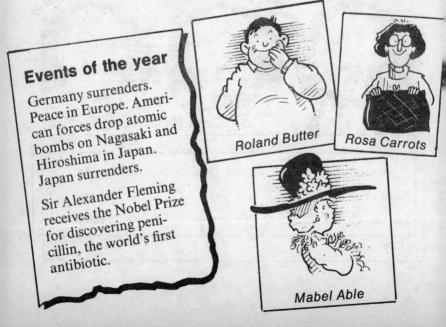

Events of the year

Germany surrenders. Peace in Europe. American forces drop atomic bombs on Nagasaki and Hiroshima in Japan. Japan surrenders.

Sir Alexander Fleming receives the Nobel Prize for discovering penicillin, the world's first antibiotic.

Roland Butter

Rosa Carrots

Mabel Able

To celebrate the end of the war, the residents of Rose Terrace are having a street party!

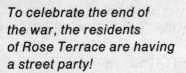

Ivor Loaf, the local baker, has made a special victory cake . . .

and the town band is

providing the entertainment!!

But look –

the cake has been stolen!!!

One of these suspects stole the cake . . . but which one?

If you choose . . .	Secret Message letter	Next go to . . .
Roland Butter	E	1953
Mable Able	A	1985
Rosa Carrots	I	1969

1946

'I'm starving,' moaned Anna. 'Me, too,' said Ryan. 'Can we have something to eat?'

Grandpa scratched his head. 'That might be a bit difficult. For a start, in 1946 you still had to buy your food with ration coupons – and we don't have any of those. Anyway, there wasn't much to eat at the best of times.'

'What about those boxes?' suggested Ryan, pointing to a pile of crates, 'Look, some of them are full of bananas.'

'Ooh, I'd love a banana,' groaned Anna, and she reached out to open one of the boxes. Grandpa stopped her just in time.

Events of the year

The first plane takes off from 'Heath Row' airport, west of London.

The first biro pens, invented by Hungarian Ladislao Biro, go on sale.

The first bananas to be seen since the war arrive in Britain – and a four-year-old girl dies after eating too many of them too quickly.

American scientists report a link between smoking and lung cancer.

'Hold on, there's a message written on that label,' he said, looking closer. 'That's very odd – it seems to be in a foreign language.'

This is what Grandpa saw. Can you work out what it means and make a choice? You'll need a pencil and paper!

NIOG NABG SANA
OENO EHTF OBES ISEX LUFS BFOL NANA NO.SA NOCE
NIAT OBAS HT.BM SERE ERAT TPME EHTY ANAB ASAN
NIER ERGA XOBY DEIT HTIW IRTS NAGN TIWD UNAH
DISP WODE BALN HT.LE MOBE ISIB EHTN WGIB ETIH
EXOB EBAL DELL ANAB .SAN

If you choose . . .	Secret Message letter	Next go to . . .
The big white box labelled BANANAS	B	1957
The black box tied with rope	T	1964
The grey box with the upside-down label	N	1982

1947

'Hold on tight, kids!' cried Grandpa, grabbing the rudder as a big wave swept across the sea towards them. 'Oh, a life on the ocean wave . . .' he began to sing.

'Euuughhh,' moaned Anna. 'I hate sailing. We'd better find land soon – otherwise I'm going to be sick.'

Ryan grabbed hold of a rope and looked up at the sign on top of the boat. '*Kon-Tiki*,' he read aloud. 'What does that mean?'

'As far as I can remember,' answered Grandpa, 'the *Kon-Tiki* was built by a chap called Thor Heyerdahl. He had this theory that thousands of years ago people sailed from South America all the way to Polynesia on rafts made of balsa-wood. Everyone thought he was barmy, so he built a raft himself and set off to prove it was possible.'

Events of the year

Terrible snowstorms cut off towns and villages. Instead of bombs, the RAF drops food parcels.

The phrase 'flying saucers' is used to describe Unidentified Flying Objects for the first time.

'And did he get there?' asked Ryan.

'Yes, eventually, after lots of adventures,' said Grandpa.

'Land ahoy!' gasped Anna, pointing ahead. 'Hurray, I can see some islands –'

'And I can see some sharks!' yelled Ryan.

'*And* we're beginning to sink!' Grandpa cried.

The *Kon-Tiki* Challenge
Your challenge is to steer a safe course through all the hazards and land on one of the three islands. The boat is already beginning to sink, so you've only got time for 12 moves. Each move must be in a straight line left, right, up or down, linking the dots; no diagonal lines are allowed. Which island will you land on?

If you choose ...	Secret Message letter	Next go to ...
Skull Island	F	1971
Treasure Island	L	1952
Devil's Island	R	1947

1948

'1948 smells horrible,' said Anna.

'I know what it is,' said Ryan unhappily. 'Disinfectant! It smells just like the hospital my mum took me to when I broke my arm. I had to have an injection.'

'It's a hospital all right,' said Grandpa. 'Let's hop up on this trolley and go for a spin.' Anna and Ryan climbed aboard and Grandpa pushed off. They went scooting down the corridor. 'Whoopee!' they shouted.

'But why are we in a hospital?' Ryan asked as they rattled along.

'Because Merlin knows that 1948 was the year the National Health Service started,' chuckled Grandpa. 'Before then, if you got ill, you had to go and pay the doctor to make you better.'

Anna looked surprised. 'What if you didn't have any money?'

Events of the year

Colonel 'Chuck' Yeager becomes the first person to fly faster than the speed of sound.

The Olympics are held in London.

The first electronic transistors are put into radios.

Prince Charles is born.

The state of Israel is founded.

'Then it was difficult to get any medicine,' said Grandpa. 'The NHS was a big improvement – even if they *do* keep giving you injections!' At that moment, the trolley did an emergency stop all on its own and Grandpa's glasses fell off. 'I think Merlin's in charge of the brakes,' he muttered.

To the right and left were the doors to two wards. And on the wall ahead was a notice that read:

Hospital Challenge

Fore Ward and Back Ward seem at first sight to be identical. But if you look closely, you'll see a number of differences. How many differences can you spot?

If you choose ...	Secret Message letter	Next go to ...
10 differences	E	1955
13 differences	I	1966
15 differences	A	1978

1949

The next thing they knew, they were standing in a busy market. 'Look what Grandpa's got!' Anna laughed, pointing to the shopping-bag he was holding.

'And I've got the shopping-list,' said Ryan, holding it out to read. 'Vegetables, socks and sweets.'

Anna jingled something in her pocket. 'Is this real money?' she asked, pulling out a handful of strange coins. 'Look at these big brown coins – and that funny little one there.'

'It's a threepenny bit!' exclaimed Grandpa, turning the coins over. 'And look, a farthing, and here's a shilling.'

Anna and Ryan were puzzled. 'But there are no ten or fifty pence pieces,' they protested.

'That's because this is the old currency,' explained

Events of the year

The first small 'single' records, played at 45 r.p.m., go on sale in the USA.

Chocolate and sweet rationing ends – but only for a few months.

BBC television broadcasts the first weather forecast.

London's first launderette opens.

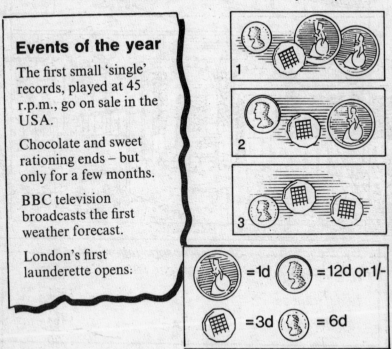

Grandpa. 'It was replaced by the new decimal coins in 1971. Until then, we used coins like these. There were twelve pence to a shilling and 24 shillings in a pound.'

'Weird,' said Anna, shaking her head.

'Who cares,' cried Ryan, 'just as long as we can buy some sweets! The shopping-list says we've got to buy a big bar of chocolate and a packet of mints.' They looked at the sweet-stall – and realized that it wasn't going to be *that* easy . . .

Chocolate Challenge
From the information in the picture, work out what the price of a large bar of chocolate and a packet of mints would be. Then choose which coins will pay for them exactly.

SPECIAL OFFER

Large Bar Chocolate 10d
1 Bar of Toffee + 1 box
of Jelly babies 1/-
1 Box of Jelly Babies +
1 Packet of Mints 7d
1 Large Bar of Chocolate +
1 Box of Jelly Babies 1/3d
1 Large Bar of Chocolate
+ 1 Packet of Mints

CHOCOLATE

MINTS   MINTS   MINTS

If you choose . . .	Secret Message letter	Next go to . . .
1	K	1961
2	P	1979
3	N	1990

1950

Suddenly they were standing outside a huge house with stone gargoyles looking down on them. 'Luvaduck Hall,' read Anna, spotting a sign above the door.

'And look at this,' said Ryan, pointing down at the path. Someone had written a word using bits of stick. WHODUNNIT? it said.

Grandpa chuckled. 'There's our message from Merlin!'

'But who's done what?' asked Anna, puzzled.

At that moment, the door opened silently before them.

'I think we're about to find out,' whispered Grandpa. Quietly, the three of them walked in.

In the great hall Lord Luvaduck was sitting in a big chair. Beside him sat Lady Luvaduck, sobbing into her lace-trimmed hankie. Across the room stood the upright figure of Laurence the butler, and beside him stood Lily the maid. Seated on another chair was the Luvaducks' guest, the lovely Lydia Languid, twisting a hankie in her hands.

'You all know why I've asked you to come here,' said Lord Luvaduck sternly. 'A few hours ago, my wife went to her room and discovered that her priceless diamond necklace had been stolen. You three were the only people in the house at the time, and therefore you are all suspects.'

'Ohhh, my beautiful diamonds!' wailed Lady Luvaduck.

Lord Luvaduck patted her gently on the shoulder.

'We'll soon have them back, my dear,' he said. 'Now, Lily, when did you last go into her ladyship's bedroom?'

'This afternoon, my lord,' said Lily, stepping forward. As she did so she brushed past Ryan, who held his nose.

'Whew!' he muttered. 'What a terrible pong – it's like apples mixed with bonfire smoke.'

'I went in there to put two handkerchiefs and her ladyship's new bottle of Autumn Ecstasy perfume on the dressing-table,' explained Lily. 'The diamonds were there, lying in their velvet box.'

'Thank you, Lily,' said Lord Luvaduck. 'Now, Laurence, what about you?'

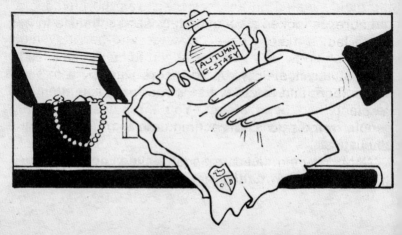

Laurence looked most offended. 'I am a butler, m'lord, not a lady's maid. I *never*, ever go into her ladyship's room.'

'But Laurence,' interrupted Lady Luvaduck, 'don't you remember that yesterday I sent you to my room to catch a spider?'

'Oh, yes,' said Laurence, going red. 'I'd forgotten about that.'

Anna frowned. 'He hasn't got a very good memory, has he?' she murmured.

Lord Luvaduck nodded. 'And now our guest, Lydia. Perhaps you could tell me when *you* last went into her ladyship's room.'

Miss Languid dabbed at her forehead with her hankie. 'I haven't been in her ladyship's bedroom all day, but I did see Laurence coming out of the door,' she revealed, before sitting down again.

'Hmmm,' whispered Grandpa, 'that hankie she's holding looks a bit familiar.'

Lord Luvaduck seemed confused by what he'd heard. 'Just answer me one question,' he said. 'Did you steal her ladyship's diamond necklace?'

'No,' said Miss Languid.

'Oh yes she did,' said Lily.

'Lily is wrong,' said Laurence.

Events of the year

England is thrown out of the World Cup after losing to the USA 1–0.

The first self-service Sainsbury's store opens.

The bowler hat celebrates its 100th birthday.

The first kidney transplant occurs.

'Well, I don't know which of you is the culprit,' sighed Lord Luvaduck, 'but I'm sure *someone* can work it out.'

Diamond Challenge

It's up to you. Did Lydia, Laurence or Lily steal the necklace? Only one of them is telling the truth — the other two are lying. Who is the thief?

If you choose . . .	Secret Message letter	Next go to . . .
Lydia	D	1974
Laurence	N	1990
Lily	L	1949

1951

'Oooooooo!' Anna, Ryan and Grandpa screamed as the roller-coaster went thundering down a huge dip. 'Wheee!' they shouted as it came up the other side.

'My knees have gone all wobbly,' said Grandpa, as he staggered out of the carriage when the ride eventually came to a halt.

'And my stomach's gone all wobbly,' groaned Ryan.

Grandpa was looking around at the funfair and, beyond that, at all the strange buildings. 'I know where we are,' he told them. 'This must be the Festival of Britain. It was a sort of exhibition about new ideas and discoveries – and if I'm right, we must be in 1951.'

'I don't care what year it is,' cried Anna, jumping up and down. 'I just want to go on the dodgem cars. They're over there. Come on!'

'Hold on a minute,' said Ryan, stopping to look at a huge painting on a wall. Across the top of it was written the question WHERE NEXT? Lying on the ground were some large pieces that had fallen off the wall. 'I know,' said Anna, 'it's like a giant jigsaw!'

Events of the year

The first photograph of a yeti's footprint is taken in the Himalayan mountains.

The first LP (long-playing) records go on sale.

Margaret Roberts, one day to become Margaret Thatcher, is a candidate in a general election for the first time.

Jigsaw Puzzle

Can you work out where the three time-travellers are supposed to go?

where Next?

If you choose . . .	Secret Message letter	Next go to . . .
The Big Wheel	O	1977
The Treewalk	M	1944
The Dome of Discovery	T	1980

1952

'Hey, we're in a plane,' exclaimed Ryan, looking out of the window at fluffy white clouds. At that moment, the plane began to descend. They broke through the clouds and below them they saw blue sea and, in the distance, a huge statue.

'That's the Statue of Liberty,' said Anna. 'We learned about it at school.'

'In that case, we must be going to New York!' cried Ryan excitedly.

Grandpa reached out for the magazine stuck in a pocket on the seat in front of him. WELCOME TO THE WORLD'S FIRST 'TOURIST CLASS' AIRLINE, it read. A piece of paper slipped out of the magazine and landed on Anna's lap.

'I recognize this handwriting,' she said immediately. 'We've got another message from Merlin.'

Welcome to New York, time-travellers!
Like all tourists, you'll want to climb the Statue of Liberty.
While you're there, look out for me. I'll be in disguise,
but if you're very observant you'll be able to spot me!

Events of the year

King George VI dies and his daughter, Princess Elizabeth, becomes Queen Elizabeth II.

Zebra crossings are equipped with flashing orange beacons for the first time.

The world's longest-running play, *The Mousetrap* by Agatha Christie, opens in London.

Spot the Wizard

When Ryan, Anna and Grandpa went to visit the Statue of Liberty, there was a big crowd there. Somewhere among all the people, Merlin is hiding. First find him, then say who is standing on his right-hand side.

If you choose . . .	Secret Message letter	Next go to . . .
A man leaning over the rail	G	1965
A girl with an ice-cream	H	1983
A woman with a baby	F	1991

1953

'This is a real treat!' chuckled Grandpa, looking around with wide-open eyes. 'I'll say this for Merlin – he sends us to some of the best places.'

'But why are we waiting outside this church?' asked Ryan, bewildered.

'And why are there soldiers everywhere, and people cheering?' chipped in Anna.

'Because it's Coronation Day,' beamed Grandpa, 'and this is no ordinary church, it's Westminster Abbey. And here comes the Queen! Hurray!'

Sure enough, there was the noise of hoofs clattering on cobbles and into view came a cavalcade of horses, followed by a magnificent golden coach. It drew up

It's Coronation Day . . .

outside the Abbey and the Queen began to get out, but suddenly a very worried-looking man came running forward, waving his arms in the air.

'The crown has been stolen!' he cried. 'Without it the coronation can't go on!'

Grandpa, Ryan and Anna looked knowingly at each other. 'It sounds to me,' said Ryan, 'as if Merlin's been up to his old tricks again.'

'And I bet it's up to us to sort it out,' nodded Anna.

The Coronation Mystery
If you study the words and pictures carefully, you'll discover who stole the crown.

. . . and everyone is preparing for the ceremony.

The Keeper of the Jewels is fetching the crown . . .

Events of the year

Sir Edmund Hillary and Sherpa Tensing Norgay from Nepal become the first men to reach the top of Mount Everest.

Thanks to television, millions of people can now watch the coronation ceremony.

Stiletto-heeled shoes become fashionable for the first time.

. . . but the crown has gone!!!

There are only three suspects. Which one of them stole the crown???

If you choose . . .	Secret Message letter	Next go to . . .
The Archbishop of Yorkbury	K	1968
General Hardware	E	1972
The Prime Minister	Y	1988

1954

'Where on earth has Merlin sent us *now*?' grumbled Grandpa. The three of them were crouched in what seemed like a little cave, except that a strange orange light was shining in from all sides and making them all look ill.

'It's f-f-f-f-freezing,' stuttered Ryan, rubbing his arms.

'Ouch!' said Grandpa, as he tried to stand up and bashed his head on the roof. The roof moved a bit and there was a sliding noise.

'I know what's happened,' Anna exclaimed, 'we must be in a tent! Yes – here's the way out.' She unzipped a zipper and daylight flooded in. She and Grandpa looked out. All around them the landscape was covered with snow and above them towered rocky mountain peaks. The tent was covered with a layer of snow, too, but some of it had slid off when Grandpa had tried to stand up. 'We could be anywhere,' sighed Anna.

'The Alps?' suggested Grandpa. 'Or the Rocky Mountains?'

'I've found something,' said Ryan's voice from inside. 'I think we're in the Him . . . the Him . . . Oh, it's no good, I can't pronounce it.'

'The Himalayas,' said Grandpa, reading the old newspaper that Ryan had found. 'Listen to this, you two. It's dated January 1954. "A group of experts have gone to the Himalayas to capture a yeti. This elusive creature, known also as the Abominable Snowman, has never been caught."'

Ryan laughed. 'There's no such thing as an Abominable Snowman.' But that moment, Anna gave a little shriek and dived back into the tent.

'What's wrong?' asked Grandpa.

'There are some things moving out there – and they're big and hairy with pink eyes!'

The Yeti Hunt

How many Abominable Snowmen can you see hidden in this picture? They are good at hiding themselves, so count carefully.

Events of the year

Roger Bannister becomes the first person to run a mile in less than four minutes.

IBM introduce the first office 'computer', though it can't do half the things a modern personal computer can do.

Elvis Presley releases his first record.

If you choose . . .	Secret Message letter	Next go to . . .
6 yetis	V	1989
8 yetis	G	1942
12 yetis	B	1973

1955

'I must be imagining things,' said Grandpa. 'I thought I saw a giant mouse.'

'You *did*, Grandpa,' shouted Anna, jumping up and down with excitement. 'Mickey Mouse! Over there.' Sure enough, there was Mickey Mouse, shaking hands with people.

'Thank goodness,' sighed Grandpa with relief. 'Your grandma's always telling me I'm mad, and I was beginning to wonder if she was right!'

'I know where we are!' laughed Anna, and she was so pleased, she did a cartwheel. Just then a parade came by, with a marching band and cheerleaders and a big banner reading, DISNEYLAND GRAND OPENING, 18 JULY 1955.

Ryan couldn't stop smiling. 'Good old Merlin,' he cried. 'I always wanted to come to Disneyland, and now I'm here!'

They spent all day enjoying the rides, without coming across a single puzzle to solve. It was late afternoon by the time they walked up to the fairy-tale castle. They were just entering through the gates, when Anna spotted a flag fluttering on the flagpole. 'Look, there are words on that flag,' she said. Grandpa helped to undo the ropes and pull the flag down.

Events of the year

Commercial television is broadcast for the first time, and the first advert is for S R toothpaste.

In America a man called Ray Kroc buys a drive-in hamburger restaurant from the two McDonald brothers, and starts to turn it into the biggest fast-food business in the world.

The first edition of *The Guinness Book of Records* is published.

This is what was written on it:

The Tower Puzzle
At the top of the page you can see a flat pattern for a castle tower. Which of the three towers does it match up with?

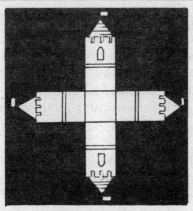

If you choose . . .	Secret Message letter	Next go to . . .
A	Y	1969
B	A	1985
C	O	1945

1956

The next thing, the three time-travellers found themselves standing in a long corridor. 'What are we supposed to do?' asked Ryan.

'I don't know,' said Grandpa, with a shrug.

Anna walked down the corridor. 'Someone called Ernie is working in here,' she called. 'It's got his name on the door. Maybe he can help us.' She knocked and opened the door a few inches.

'He's not here,' she said. The room was almost filled by a huge black machine covered in criss-crossing wires and valves, and every few seconds it began to shake and lights began to flash all over it. Then a ribbon of paper came out of a slot – and just as suddenly it stopped again.

'Maybe there's a message on the paper ribbon,' suggested Ryan, and he picked up one end to check. 'No,' he said, 'it's nothing but numbers.'

Meanwhile Grandpa had been walking round, looking at things. Now he pointed to the top of the machine. 'Look up there,' he said, and the children saw the letters ERNIE stamped on to the machine.

'So the *machine*'s called Ernie!' laughed Anna. 'Why give a machine a name?'

'Because it's special,' said Grandpa. 'You see, it's actually called Electrical Random Number Indicator Equipment. E,R,N,I,E. It prints out random numbers.'

'Why does anyone need a load of numbers?' asked Ryan.

'For Premium Bonds!' said Grandpa. 'In 1956 the Post Office started selling Premium Bonds. Whenever you buy a bond, it has a number on it. If Ernie here comes up with the same number as your bond, *bingo* – you win some money.'

At that moment, Ernie began to rumble extra loudly,

and with a big hiccup a great torrent of paper ribbon
came spilling on to the floor.

'I've a feeling that Ernie's just delivered our next
puzzle,' said Ryan.

Ernie's Puzzle
*See how many times you can find the word ERNIE
hidden in this grid. It may be written across, down or
diagonally, either forwards or backwards, but always in
a straight line. If you've got a pencil and ruler, they'll
come in useful.*

P	B	R	E	R	N	I	E	B	O
R	O	E	B	E	I	N	R	E	N
E	N	R	O	E	B	O	N	I	D
M	E	N	N	E	E	E	I	N	E
I	E	I	D	R	D	E	E	R	B
U	E	E	N	N	E	N	N	E	O
M	E	I	E	R	O	I	O	E	N
E	E	R	N	I	E	B	N	B	D
P	R	E	M	U	I	M	E	R	P
F	I	N	R	E	B	O	N	D	E

**vents of
e year**

he first video-
pe recording
achine is
emonstrated.

The government
passes a law
allowing
television to
start at 6 p.m.
instead of 7 p.m.

If you choose . . .	Secret Message letter	Next go to . . .
6	W	1963
11	L	1975
17	S	1984

1957

'Ten, nine, eight . . .' Colonel Coustard of the Cape Canoodle Space Centre started the countdown. Anna, Ryan and Grandpa watched through the huge glass windows of the control room as the rocket on the launch pad began to rumble. Smoke and flickers of flame began to appear from its base. Through a little porthole near the tip of the rocket, they could see the wagging tail of Sandy, who was about to become the world's first Labrador in space.

'Three, two, one,' counted Colonel Coustard, 'lift off!' Everyone in the control centre held their breath, waiting for the rocket to take off. But nothing happened. 'Abandon launch,' instructed the Colonel. He walked across the tarmac to inspect the rocket and see what had gone wrong.

A few minutes later he was back, carrying a bit of broken metal. 'Look at this,' he said, holding it out. 'Someone has cut the rocket sprocket in half. We've been sabotaged!'

Grandpa winked at Anna and Anna winked at Ryan. 'I think,' whispered Grandpa, 'we have another mystery to solve.'

Meanwhile Colonel Coustard was thinking hard. 'I checked the sprocket twenty minutes before the count-down started, so that narrows down the suspects. There was Morris Major, our space expert, Doris Dainty, who trained Sandy the Labrador for his mission, and Boris Borisovitch, the technician who was supposed to check all the equipment. And there's one more clue.' From his pocket he took a few strands of bright blue wool. 'This was caught on one of the rocket levers. Whoever the saboteur was, they must have been wearing something blue. Let's call in the suspects.'

The first was Morris Major, wearing a tweed suit and tie. 'How dare you suggest that I, the world's greatest space expert, would sabotage my own rocket,' he pro-tested. 'You should arrest that Russian, Boris, im-mediately. He's a spy!'

'Have you and Boris had another argument?' asked Colonel Coustard.

'He's a blithering idiot!' blustered Morris Major. 'Why,

only a few minutes ago I had to let him out of the loo. The fool had locked himself in! And now he's gone and ruined my attempt to send a rocket to the planet Andorra.'

'Hmm,' said Colonel Coustard. 'One last question. Do you own a blue woolly jumper?'

'Certainly not,' snapped Morris Major, and he left the room.

Next came Doris Dainty, dressed in pink and with Sandy the Labrador bouncing at her side. 'Mrs Dainty, are you very fond of Sandy?' asked the Colonel.

'Yes,' said Doris, patting the dog. 'It nearly broke my heart when I had to take him aboard that rocket. I didn't want to see poor Sandy zooming into space all on his own. I'm pleased the rocket didn't take off.'

'What did you do once you had put Sandy aboard the rocket?'

'I was going to drive home,' said Mrs Dainty, 'but my car wouldn't start, and I'm hopeless at anything mechanical – my husband says I wouldn't know the difference between a hub-cap and a carburettor.'

'You can go now,' said Colonel Coustard. 'Boris Borisovitch, please.'

The door opened and in came a very scruffy-looking man with his hair unbrushed and a button missing from his shirt. 'What's this I hear about you getting shut in the loo?' asked the Colonel.

'Someone locked me in! I banged and shouted for

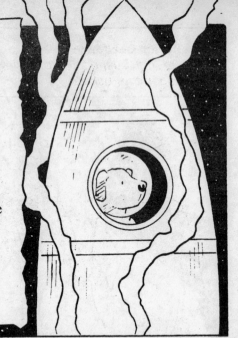

fifteen minutes and eventually that so-called space expert Morris came and opened it.'

'You don't believe he is an expert?' asked Colonel Coustard.

'He says he is, but he doesn't even know the names of the planets,' grumbled Boris. 'Mercury, Venus, Mars, Jupiter, Saturn . . . *I'm* more of a space expert than he is.'

'A final question,' said the Colonel. 'Do you own a blue jumper?'

'Yes,' said Boris. 'I was wearing a blue jumper this morning, but it was so hot I took it off.'

'I see,' said Colonel Coustard. 'I think I've heard all I need to know.'

'And we have too,' nodded Grandpa and Ryan. But have *you*?

The Rocket Challenge
Two of the suspects are telling the truth – but who sabotaged the rocket?

BORIS   MORRIS   DORIS

If you choose . . .	Secret Message letter	Next go to . . .
Morris	D	1943
Doris	S	1970
Boris	N	1987

1958

'Mmmmm, hamburgers!' exclaimed Anna and Ryan, grabbing one each.

'I think I'd prefer a hot dog,' said Grandpa, reaching out for one. As they ate, all three time-travellers looked at the scene around them. The place was really in a terrible mess. There were all sorts of things stacked up on top of each other, while animals wandered about among them.

'Where are we?' Ryan asked Grandpa.

Grandpa didn't know. But before they could begin to explore, there was a loud noise as if someone had switched on a giant hairdrier, and a strange vehicle came floating across the ground with a man aboard. He waved at them and pulled up near by. When he turned the vehicle off, it sank to the ground with a sighing sound.

Events of the year

Michael Jackson is born on 29 August.

The first yellow 'no parking' lines are painted in British streets and parking meters appear in London; drivers don't like them!

Britain's first motorway, an eight-mile stretch near Preston, opens.

People fly in hang-gliders for the first time.

'That must be a hovercraft,' said Anna. 'Mum and I went to France on one last year.'

'You're absolutely right, young lady,' nodded the man. 'It's a hovercraft and it was invented in 1958.' He reached into his pocket and took out a letter. 'I was asked to give you this,' he announced, handing it over, and before they could say anything, he was off again.

'This looks like Merlin's handwriting,' said Anna as she opened the envelope. And this was what she found inside.

The H Challenge
Hello, time-travellers,
If you look around you'll see lots of things beginning
with the letter H. How many are there exactly? Happy
counting! Love, Merlin.

If you choose . . .	Secret Message letter	Next go to . . .
15	H	1980
24	I	1951
30	E	1962

1959

'Watch out, Grandpa!' squealed Anna from the back seat of the car they had just materialized in. Grandpa, who was sitting behind the steering-wheel, braked and brought the car safely to a halt outside a factory building.

'Phew!' he breathed. 'We might have had an accident. I don't know what that Merlin thinks he's doing, but this is getting dangerous!'

Just then the passenger door opened, and who should stick his head in but Merlin himself. 'Terribly sorry about that,' he said. 'I had a bit of a mix-up with my time and space differentials! Now I'm here, I'll explain the next challenge.' Anna, Ryan and Grandpa climbed out.

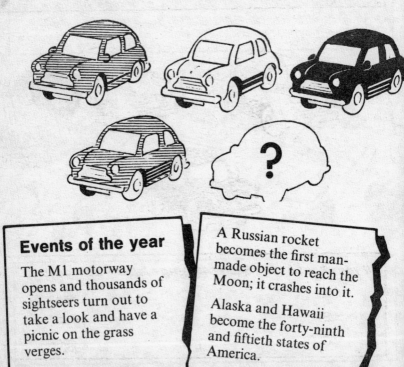

Events of the year

The M1 motorway opens and thousands of sightseers turn out to take a look and have a picnic on the grass verges.

A Russian rocket becomes the first man-made object to reach the Moon; it crashes into it.

Alaska and Hawaii become the forty-ninth and fiftieth states of America.

'It's a Mini,' said Grandpa, looking at the exterior of the car.

'They're *all* Minis,' observed Ryan, seeing dozens of cars lined up outside the factory.

'That's right,' said Merlin cheerfully. 'It's the first Mini factory.'

'I used to have a Mini myself,' said Grandpa. 'A nice red one.'

'In that case you should find this puzzle easy,' said Merlin, 'because it's all about Minis.'

A Mini Challenge
Here is a series of four Mini cars. Which of the cars below should come next – A, B or C?

If you choose . . .	Secret Message letter	Next go to . . .
A	C	1948
B	N	1981
C	G	1966

1960

The next thing they knew, Ryan, Anna and Grandpa found themselves on a balcony overlooking a busy street. 'Look,' cried Ryan, pointing to the cars below, 'there's a traffic warden about to give someone a parking ticket.'

'And another one there,' pointed Anna.

As she was speaking, a strong gust of wind whirled down the street, making the traffic wardens hold on hard to their hats. One of the parking tickets fell out of their hands and flew up to the balcony, where Grandpa caught it.

'I bet it's a message from Merlin,' said Anna, and she was right. This was what it said:

The Parking Ticket Challenge
In 1960 the first traffic wardens started patrolling London's streets. On their first day they handed out 344 parking tickets to motorists. How many parking tickets can you see in this picture?

Events of the year

Wilma Rudolph of the USA wins three Olympic gold sprinting medals, despite the fact that she had had polio and couldn't walk until she was eight years old.

The first laser is demonstrated. The word 'LASER' stands for Light Amplification by Stimulated Emission of Radiation.

If you choose . . .	Secret Message letter	Next go to . . .
9	P	1986
11	J	1954
14	N	1942

1961

'Grandpa, look at all the puppies!' As Anna crouched down to stroke one of the black-spotted puppies, more rushed over to her, wagging their tails.

Ryan was already sitting on the ground with puppies climbing all over him, trying to lick his ears. 'Don't you like dogs?' he asked, noticing that Grandpa didn't look pleased.

'No,' said Grandpa grumpily. 'They come into my garden and dig up my best cabbages.' He looked down. A puppy with a spot over one eye was begging for a cuddle. Reluctantly, Grandpa picked it up. It wriggled in his arms, nibbling his fingers. 'Well,' said Grandpa, after he had tickled its tummy for a few minutes, 'I suppose *some* dogs aren't too bad.'

'I wonder how many there are,' said Anna. 'They each have a number on their collar. This one is number 16 . . .'

'And this is number 51,' announced Ryan.

'And this is number 99,' said Grandpa, inspecting the collar of the puppy he was holding. At that moment, two larger dogs came bounding up. '99 puppies and two parents makes 101 altogether,' he mused, 'and I'm no expert, but I'd say all these dogs are Dalmatians . . .'

'*101 Dalmatians!*' chorused Anna and Ryan. 'We saw a cartoon about them.' Just then one of the grown-up dogs came over with something in its mouth. Ryan held out his hand and the dog dropped what it was carrying.

'Listen to this,' he said. 'It's a spotty dog challenge!'

The Spotty Dog Challenge
Two of these spotty dogs have identical markings. Which two?

If you choose . . .	Secret Message letter	Next go to . . .
6 and 19	L	1946
11 and 16	K	1982
5 and 12	U	1979

1962

'That's funny,' said Anna, 'I'm sure I didn't have this in my pocket a few minutes ago.' She pulled out an envelope and looked at the address. 'What shall we do? We can't deliver it – we don't even know where we are, so we can't tell where Mill Cottage is.'

Grandpa pointed across the street. 'There's a town map over there,' he suggested. 'Let's have a look.'

They crossed the road and inspected the map, but Anna shook her head. 'This is ridiculous,' she complained. 'It doesn't even give the names of the roads. We can't work out an answer from this!'

But Ryan had been thinking quietly to himself. 'I think *I* can do it,' he said. Can you too?

Events of the year

The first push-button street crossings, named pelican crossings, come into use.

An American frogman swims the English Channel – underwater.

An Essex schoolboy claims a world record after dancing the Twist non-stop for thirty-three hours.

The *Sunday Times* issues the first colour supplement.

GORDON BENNETT
MILL COTTAGE,
PARKVIEW CRESCENT,
PUDDLEBY.

TOWN HALL

The Letter Challenge

Using the map on the wall, see if you can work out where Gordon Bennett lives. Then work out the shortest route to get to his house. What's the least number of roads you have to cross to get there?

If you choose . . .	Secret Message letter	Next go to . . .
2	F	1951
4	D	1980
5	G	1944

1963

'We haven't got to watch Shakespeare, have we?' Ryan asked, looking around at the packed theatre in which they'd suddenly arrived. 'Yuck, boring.'

Grandpa smiled. 'No need to worry about Shakespeare, lad. Look up in that box over there. You too, Anna.'

'It's the Queen!' they both whispered instantly.

'I wouldn't mind betting that Merlin's sent us to watch the Royal Variety Performance,' said Grandpa.

Just then the red velvet curtains parted and on to the stage walked a man with shiny hair. 'Your Majesty, my lords, ladies and gentlemen, I'm afraid I have some bad news,' he said, looking very serious. 'You came here

The Beatles are waiting to appear at the Royal Variety Performance.

tonight to hear the Beatles perform their latest hits, but unfortunately something terrible has happened and they cannot play.'

Grandpa, Anna and Ryan stood up and began to edge out of their row of seats, while the audience booed at the man on stage. 'Looks like we've got a mystery to solve,' said Grandpa, leading the children round the back of the stage to the dressing-rooms.

The Mystery of the Silent Drums
Study the words and pictures carefully and see if you can work out who the culprit is!

Events of the year

Beatlemania sweeps Britain and the USA.

The Great Train Robbers steal more than £2 million after holding up a mail train.

President John Kennedy of the USA is assassinated.

TV viewers see a woman read the news for the first time.

Only three people can have stolen them: Ollie Slick, the comedian; Isla Moppit, the cleaner; and Terry Belldin, rival drummer of 'The Crash' band.

All three suspects had their pockets searched, but the drumsticks weren't found. Can you solve the mystery? Who took them?

If you choose . . .	Secret Message letter	Next go to . . .
Ollie Slick	R	1952
Isla Moppit	F	1947
Terry Belldin	M	1971

1964

'Well, shiver me timbers!' said a loud voice, and Grandpa, Anna and Ryan all spun round. The voice belonged to a big man with a bushy black beard and an eye-patch. He wore a flowing white shirt, with the letters DJ embroidered in red on the pocket, and big black boots. Behind him stood a crowd of other ruffians.

'Pirates!' breathed Ryan, before he could stop himself.

'That's right, my lad,' said the man with the eye-patch. 'I'm Captain Crook, leader of this gang of pirate DJs. Our mission is to steal Max Bygraves records from the BBC and fill the airwaves with rock, so the people of Britain will know what *real* music sounds like.'

'What a brilliant idea,' said Anna, but Captain Crook ignored her.

'The three of you are stowaways,' he said accusingly. 'Or spies from the Beeb who've come to blow us up.'

'Don't be silly,' said Grandpa, getting a bit cross, because he was actually rather fond of Max Bygraves records. But the Captain didn't listen.

'Take them down to the hold,' he ordered. 'They can stay there until we're ready to make them walk the plank.' And before they could do anything, Grandpa, Ryan and Anna were bundled into the depths of the creaking ship and tied up.

'If this is Merlin's idea of a joke, I don't think it's very funny,' said Grandpa.

'But what if it isn't?' said Anna, really scared. 'Who's going to get us out of here?'

Events of the year

In South Africa, Nelson Mandela is sentenced to life imprisonment for plotting against the white government.

Radio Caroline becomes the first pirate radio station, broadcasting from a ship in the North Sea.

BBC2 goes on air for the first time. The first programme shown is *Playschool*.

A Pirate Puzzle

Can you help Anna, Ryan and Grandpa escape from Captain Crook? One of them has been tied up in such a way that it's not too difficult to undo the knot. But which one?

If you choose . . .	Secret Message letter	Next go to . . .
Ryan	U	1987
Grandpa	Y	1943
Anna	I	1957

1965

'Out of this world!' cried Anna, turning a somersault and bumping gently into the space capsule, before floating off again. Ryan came past, swimming in space as if he was in the pool. 'Aren't you coming out for a spacewalk?' he asked Grandpa, who was staying firmly put in the capsule.

'No thanks,' said Grandpa, trying not to look down at the Earth, glowing all blue and green hundreds of miles beneath them. 'I like something firm under my feet.'

'But you can't fall,' shouted Anna, as she floated upside down. 'There's no gravity.'

Just then another spacecraft came into view and out

Events of the year

Colonel Alexei Leonev takes the first 'walk' in space. Not long after, an American astronaut, Major Edward White, does the same thing.

A map proving that Christopher Columbus was not the first person to discover America is published, showing that the Vikings got there 400 years before him.

floated two more spacemen, trailing long airlines that kept them supplied with oxygen. As they floated around, the computer aboard the space capsule began to flash, and a few seconds later a message came up on the screen.

'Look at this, kids,' said Grandpa, as Ryan and Anna floated back into the capsule. 'We've got our next challenge.'

A Space Challenge
One of these spacemen has a longer airline than the other. How long is it? Every metre in length is marked with a cross, so get counting!

If you choose . . .	Secret Message letter	Next go to . . .
9 metres	V	1991
12 metres	N	1976

1966

'England, England, England!' chanted the thousands of football fans lined up on the terraces. Ryan joined in loudly. On the scoreboard opposite the spot where they were standing, the score read England 3 West Germany 2. Grandpa's face lit up. 'Do you know where Merlin's sent us now? We're at the 1966 World Cup Final – England's finest footballing moment. Come on, England!' he shouted.

'Calm down, Grandpa,' said Anna, who thought football was pretty boring. 'Are we going to win?' As she spoke, a player in a red shirt came tearing down one side of the pitch and blasted the ball in the back of the net. The England fans went wild, throwing hats and programmes into the air, and Grandpa and Ryan went bananas. Anna didn't go crazy though. She was too busy reading the latest challenge, which was written on a scarf that had fallen at her feet.

'What sort of puzzle is it?' asked Grandpa, when at last the World Cup had been presented to the England captain and the fans had left the stadium.

'It's a football puzzle,' said Anna, 'and I think I've already solved it.' Can *you*?

The World Cup Puzzle

Six teams will reach the final rounds of the 1994 World Cup. You can work out where they'll finish by following these clues.

England will do better than Argentina, but not as well as Italy.
Brazil will lose the championship by only one point.
West Germany will finish ahead of Argentina.
England will come fourth in the championship.
The Dutch will be unbeaten.

Which order will they finish in?

'Here's my solution,' said Anna, holding out her score-card.

'And here's mine,' said Ryan.

'And here's mine,' said Grandpa. Which one of them got it right?

Events of the year

140 people are killed in the Aberfan disaster in Wales after a slag heap slips down a hill and buries the local school under thousands of tonnes of coal and rubble. More than 116 of the dead are children.

1. HOLLAND
2. BRAZIL
3. ITALY
4. ENGLAND
5. W. GERMANY
6. ARGENTINA.

1. W. GERMANY
2. BRAZIL
3. HOLLAND
4. ITALY
5. ENGLAND
6. ARGENTINA

1. HOLLAND
2. ITALY
3. BRAZIL
4. ENGLAND
5. W. GERMANY
6. ARGENTINA.

If you choose ...	Secret Message letter	Next go to ...
Anna	B	1955
Ryan	T	1969
Grandpa	H	1978

83

1967

'This is very nice,' said Grandpa, lying back in the sun as the boat bobbed calmly up and down. 'I wish I'd brought my sunglasses with me.' But before he could have a snooze, Anna came running over.

'I've found three wetsuits – one big one and two little ones. And there are aqualungs too! I bet the next challenge is an underwater one.'

A few seconds later, Ryan arrived clutching a tin box. 'I saw a fishing-line over the side of the boat,' he explained, 'and when I pulled it in, *this* was on the end.' They opened the lid of the box and found inside two books and a message from Merlin. The first book was called *The History of the Rinklis* and the second was *The Rinkli Dictionary*.

'It seems,' said Grandpa, after looking through the first book for a while, 'that the Rinklis were an ancient tribe, who lost their famous treasure in a shipwreck. The treasure has never been found.'

'And their language looked like this,' added Ryan, holding out a page from the dictionary.

'And we've got to dive off this boat and find the treasure,' said Anna, reading the message from Merlin. 'Come on, everyone!'

They put on the wetsuits and aqualungs and dived over the side of the boat. 'Glug-glug-glug!' said Ryan, pointing to the wreck of an ancient ship on the sea-bed. Lying to one side of it was a stone slab with a message written on it. Maybe this was the clue to where the treasure was hidden?

The Rinkli Challenge
If you can translate the Rinklis' message, you will discover where the treasure is. Not all the letters are in the Rinkli dictionary, so you'll have to guess some. Where's the treasure?

Events of the year

TV goes colour for the first time.

The first human heart transplant is carried out by Dr Christiaan Barnard.

If you choose . . .	Secret Message letter	Next go to . . .
The rum barrel	I	1956
The big cannon	O	1975
The treasure-chest	Y	1982

1968

The next thing they knew, Grandpa, Anna and Ryan found themselves in front of a huge stadium. Across the entrance was a banner with the words MEXICO OLYMPICS, 1968 emblazoned on it. 'Merlin certainly sends us to some interesting places,' said Grandpa, mopping his brow with his handkerchief.

'Let's go into the stadium and see what's happening,' suggested Anna, leading the way. It was very crowded inside, but they found some seats.

Then Ryan saw something on the floor. 'Look,' he said, holding up a yellow envelope, 'someone's dropped their photographs. What shall we do?'

'Have a look at the pictures,' Grandpa advised. 'Perhaps there'll be a snap of the person who dropped

Events of the year

At the Olympics, long-jumper Bob Beamon of the USA jumps a massive 8.90m, a record that lasts for more than twenty years.

Britain's first sextuplets are born.

In the USA, Dr Martin Luther King, leader of the black civil rights movement, is killed by a gunman.

them, and if we spot them in the crowd we can give them back.'

Ryan opened the envelope and pulled out six photos. Written on the back of one of them was a message. 'I know who *these* pictures belong to,' cried Anna. 'They're Merlin's!'

'Which can only mean one thing,' Grandpa said cheerfully. '*Another* challenge!'

> **The Olympic Challenge**
> These are the six photos Ryan found. As you can see, they were all taken at the Olympics. One photo contains an item or a detail from each of the five others. Which one?

If you choose . . .	Secret Message letter	Next go to . . .
Photo 1	F	1950
Photo 3	K	1974
Photo 5	D	1988

1969

'Ouch!' complained Grandpa, as they bounced over a bump in the tarmac. All the luggage in the airport baggage-train (because that was where Merlin had landed them) bounced with him. 'Hold on tight, you two,' he called.

'This is better than Disneyland,' laughed Anna, who was sitting on a squidgy rucksack. Just then the baggage-train pulled up near the airport terminal and all three scrambled off and stood wondering what to do next.

'Look up there,' said Ryan excitedly, pointing to a black dot in the sky. It was getting bigger by the second, and as they watched it grow, it got louder and louder until they had to put their fingers in their ears.

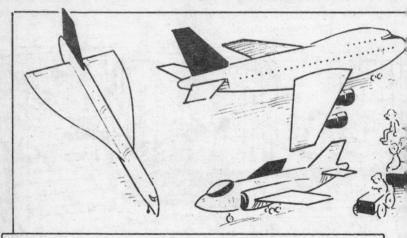

If you choose ...	Secret Message letter	Next go to ...
Patrick	B	1968
Peter	C	1972
Paul	D	1953

'It's Concorde!' they all shouted to each other as, at last, the plane came dipping gracefully down on to a runway some distance away.

'It's like a big white bird,' Ryan said admiringly, when they could hear themselves speak once more. But Grandpa wasn't listening. He was still gazing up at the sky.

'I thought I saw something else up there,' he muttered. And sure enough, there was a loud sputtering sound and out of the clouds came a much smaller plane. Behind it streamed a long banner, and as it came closer they read the words printed on it . . .

The Concorde Challenge
In the hangar you'll find three pilots and their three planes. Which pilot flies Concorde?

Patrick   Peter   Paul

Events of the year

Neil Armstrong becomes the first man to set foot on the Moon.

The maiden flight of the British Concorde takes place.

1970

Before they knew what was happening, the three time-travellers found themselves standing in the centre of a shop. Ryan gazed wonderingly at the televisions and record-players on display. 'Look at this,' he giggled, pointing to an old-fashioned tape recorder. 'It's pre-historic! Haven't they heard of Walkmans?'

'Not in 1970,' said Grandpa, seeing the date displayed on a calendar. 'It's another few years before Walkmans get invented. Or compact discs.'

By the counter was a special display. THE LATEST INVENTION – POCKET CALCULATORS read the sign. 'They call *these* pocket calculators?' Ryan asked, amazed. 'You'd need a huge pocket for one of these.'

'In 1970 people thought these calculators were amazing,' corrected Grandpa. 'They weren't to know that one day they'd be no bigger than a credit card.' All this time Anna had been staring at one particular calculator.

'This one's really weird,' she said at last. 'Some of the buttons are blank. How can you add anything up if you don't know which button's for which number?' All three of them peered at it. Scratching his head, Grandpa picked up the box and looked at the instructions on the back.

'I might have known,' he laughed. 'Merlin's been at it again!'

The Calculator Calculation
This calculator is rather special. Its buttons are numbered 1 to 9, but the numbers appear in a special order, so that whichever way you add the rows up (across, down or diagonally) they always total 15. Work out the correct number for each button, then say what the number in the middle is.

If you choose . . .	Secret Message letter	Next go to . . .
5	E	1958
2	V	1951
8	P	1962

Events of the year

The first pocket calculator is invented.

When the New English Bible is published, a million copies are sold in a single day.

1971

'If that's the Earth,' said Ryan, looking at the big blue planet spinning in the darkness, 'then we must be . . .'

'On the Moon!' concluded Grandpa. Before they could begin to explore, a moon-buggy with two astronauts aboard came chugging round some rocks. The buggy stopped and the astronauts got out and started waving their arms furiously at each other.

'We should have turned right at the big crater, not left,' one of them was shouting.

'No, we should have gone left at the meteorite, stupid,' yelled the other. 'No wonder we're lost! If we don't get back to the spacecraft Vulture, it will go back to Earth without us – and then what'll we do?'

The Moon Challenge
Whose route do you think will get the astronauts back to the spacecraft?

Events of the year

Decimal currency is introduced – goodbye to shillings, florins and half-crowns.

War in India and Pakistan as Bangladesh fights for independence.

'This sounds like a problem for us to solve,' said Grandpa. He looked around. 'This way,' he called, beckoning the children to follow him up to the top of the rocks. In the distance they could see the gleaming silvery shape of a spacecraft.

'It's easy,' cried Ryan, 'they just jump over the ravine and keep going.'

'Don't be daft,' said Grandpa, 'that's much too dangerous. If they take the right-hand fork and keep going right, they'll easily get there.'

'You're both wrong,' said Anna. 'They need to take the right-hand fork then keep going, then it's left at the rock-pile, right before the crater, then second left, left, right and then left!'

If you choose . . .	Secret Message letter	Next go to . . .
Ryan's	B	1983
Grandpa's	R	1965
Anna's	N	1952

1972

'This is *really* creepy,' shivered Anna, and her voice echoed in the darkness. Suddenly the beam from the torch lit up an eerie face looming down at them from the wall. 'Aaaargh!' they all screamed.

'It's all right,' gasped Ryan, shining the torch around. 'Don't panic, it's just a painting.'

'Whew,' said Grandpa, 'talk about making me jump!' They were standing in front of an amazing wall-painting. Around the chamber were chairs and chests and other spooky things. Anna looked at the strange writing on the wall. After a while she announced, 'Hey, I can read this! It

The Pharaoh Puzzle

Ryan is right – there is a clue that will help them choose the right door. Look for it, then decide which door to take.

says, "Welcome to the tomb of King Tootandgetout."'
Then, as she deciphered some more, her voice went a
bit wobbly. 'And it also says, "Though there are three
doors leading from my tomb, there is only one safe exit.
One door leads to a maze, where you will be lost for
ever. One door opens into a cage full of hungry lions.
One door will take you safely to the oasis. Choose
wisely."'

'There has to be *some* clue about which door to
choose,' Ryan whispered.

'Yes,' gulped Grandpa, 'there must.'

'Maybe,' groaned Anna, 'but *where*?'

Events of the year

General Idi Amin of Uganda expels 50,000 Asian people, many of whom come to England to make a new home.

The King Tutankhamun exhibition arrives in London and is immensely popular.

If you choose ...	Secret Message letter	Next go to ...
The left door	O	1950
The middle door	A	1968
The right door	I	1988

1973

A heavy smell of coffee and spices hovered in the air at the next place the time-travellers appeared. 'Smells like the mystic Orient to me,' sighed Grandpa, shutting his eyes and savouring the aroma. 'As if we were in a bazaar.'

And so they were. Around them were stalls draped with fabrics and silk carpets, trays heaped with fruit and vegetables, jewels, copper pots and pans and a million other things besides. While they were standing there, looking at everything in amazement, a little man wearing a red hat came up.

'I'm so pleased to see you,' he said. 'My name is Mustafa Biskit and my old friend Merlin said you'd be popping in. Do come and have some coffee in my shop.' So they followed him into his shop, which had a sign saying MUSTAFA BISKIT – FINE ANTIQUES over the door.

Inside they sat on cushions. Grandpa sipped strong coffee, while Ryan and Anna had orange juice. 'Merlin asked me to show you my best antique,' said Mustafa, 'so here it is. Be careful – it's very valuable.' He handed Anna a beautiful lamp, just like the one Aladdin's genie lived in.

'Is it magic?' asked Anna.

'I don't know about that,' he smiled, 'but I do know it's very, very old. Look, it's got the date marked on it. 96 BC.'

'Wow!' exclaimed Ryan. 'You mean it's genuine?'

'That's your challenge,' said Mustafa. 'Is it real – or a fake?'

Events of the year

Britain and Ireland join the European Economic Community.

J. R. R. Tolkien, creator of *The Hobbit* and *Lord of the Rings*, dies.

The Antique Expert's Challenge
It's up to you to decide whether Mustafa Biskit's lamp is a genuine antique or just a fake. What do you think?

If you choose . . .	Secret Message letter	Next go to . . .
A genuine antique	C	1956
Don't know	K	1967
A fake	T	1989

1974

'I'd do *anything* for a milk-shake and some fries,' said Ryan, with a big sigh.

'Oooh, me too,' Anna agreed, rubbing her stomach. 'What I'd really like is some pizza.'

'I'd prefer fish and chips myself,' said Grandpa wistfully. 'If we just keep walking down this street, we're sure to find a restaurant open.'

Not much further along the road, a crowd of people had gathered outside a shop and the three time-travellers stopped to see what was happening. A wide red ribbon was stretched across the front of the shop and a man wearing a gold chain round his neck was making a speech.

'Ladies and gentlemen,' he announced, 'as Mayor of Puddleby, I am honoured to declare this ultra-modern MacMackintosh fast-food restaurant open. May God bless it and all who eat in it.' With a quick snip of his golden scissors, he cut the ribbon.

'Food!' shouted Anna and Ryan, and they dragged Grandpa into the restaurant. A few minutes later they were sitting down to fried chicken and burgers and chips.

When they'd finished, Grandpa said, 'Now we've had something to eat, I suppose we'd better start looking for the next challenge.' He picked up one of the paper serviettes to wipe his hands. Its pattern caught his eye and he took a closer look and then laughed. 'We don't have to search far, though, because here it is!'

Events of the year

The first McDonald's opens in Britain.

Because of strikes and bad economic conditions, factories and offices have to close for two days a week to save energy.

The Burger Puzzle

In this puzzle, every symbol represents a different number from 1 to 6. We've added the rows and columns up so that you can see the totals. Can you work out what number the burger represents? To give you some help, milkshakes represent 4!

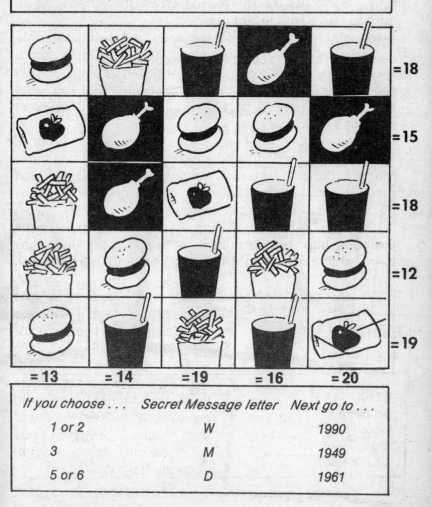

If you choose . . .	Secret Message letter	Next go to . . .
1 or 2	W	1990
3	M	1949
5 or 6	D	1961

1975

'Now we've come to China,' cried Anna. '*Blue Peter* did a programme about this place. All these statues are models of the Chinese emperor's army.'

'I'm very impressed,' said Grandpa, staring around the huge building. It was filled with row upon row of warriors, complete with horses and spears and chariots. As the three time-travellers walked round looking at them, a party of tourists came up.

'This is the Terracotta Army. Six thousand life-sized figures made around 200 BC and buried in a vast tomb,' boomed the guide. 'The workers who knew about the tomb were buried alive inside it so that it remained a secret.'

'Very nice,' said Ryan sarcastically.

'Follow me,' yelled the guide. 'Next stop, the Great

NAME: BETTY KANT
ADDRESS: 3 WAGTAIL CRES., FINCHLEY.
HOBBIES: BIRDWATCHING, HORSE RACING, KNITTING, FOREIGN LANGUAGES.

If you choose . . .	Secret Message letter	Next go to . . .
Betty	E	1963
Nick	I	1947
Wanda	A	1984

Wall.' All the tourists rushed out behind him. Grandpa, Ryan and Anna watched them go.

'Well, *they* didn't have much of a chance to see anything,' Grandpa said.

'And look,' Anna said, 'one of them has left their bag behind.' She picked it up. There was a baggage-tag round one handle and on it were these words:

The Baggage Challenge
This bag contains several items and an envelope containing details of three tourists. This bag belongs to one of them – but which one?

Anna opened the envelope and took out three cards. Then she opened the bag and tipped the contents out. It didn't take her long to work out who it should be returned to, but how long will it take you?

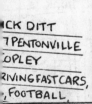

CK DITT
7 PENTONVILLE
OPLEY
RIVING FAST CARS,
FOOTBALL

NAME: WANDA ORFF
ADDRESS: 6 RETURN ROAD
DUNROAMIN SCOTLAND
HOBBIES: TRAVEL,
COOKING, PHOTOGRAPHY,
TRAMPOLINING.

Events of the year

In China the Terracotta Army is dug up by peasants looking for water.

Streaking – running around with no clothes on – becomes a craze.

1976

'I reckon we must be getting near the end of the trail now,' said Grandpa.

'Shhhh!' whispered Ryan. 'I can hear someone in the room over there. Come on.' Anna and Grandpa tiptoed silently across the polished wooden floor of the house and craned their heads round the side of the door.

An elderly lady stood in the centre of the room, looking at all the portraits on the wall in front of her. She kept sighing and shaking her head, as if she couldn't find what she was looking for.

'A damsel in distress,' said Grandpa. 'Perhaps we can help.' He opened the door and entered the room. 'Can we be of any assistance, madam?' he asked politely.

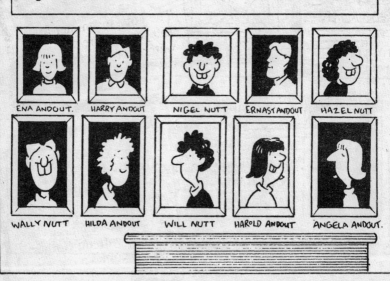

The Andout Challenge
Which of the three unnamed portraits do *you* think is Roger Andout?

ENA ANDOUT. HARRY ANDOUT NIGEL NUTT ERNEST ANDOUT HAZEL NUTT

WALLY NUTT HILDA ANDOUT WILL NUTT HAROLD ANDOUT ANGELA ANDOUT.

'Perhaps you can,' said the old lady. 'My name is Miss Burple, and though I may look like a little grey-haired old lady, I am actually a famous detective. At the moment I am trying to catch a conman called Roger Andout. Unfortunately, no one knows what he looks like, because he has never had his photo taken. I came here to Andout Hall in the hope of finding a portrait of him, but it's no good. Though there are three pictures of men of Roger's age, none of them has a name. I can't tell which one is him, so I still don't know what he looks like.'

'That certainly is a difficult problem,' said Grandpa, looking at the portraits. 'But I think there may be a way of identifying him after all . . .'

Events of the year

Agatha Christie, queen of the crime writers, dies.

The hottest summer for 250 years; there are water shortages throughout the country.

If you choose . . .	Secret Message letter	Next go to . . .
Left	P	1991
Top right	J	1991
Bottom	L	1991

1977

'And the next race will be the 1977 Grand National,' came the announcement over the loudspeakers. Around the racecourse, people began to cheer. 'The favourite for the race is the New Zealand-bred horse Wotagowa.'

Grandpa was excited. 'I wonder if Merlin would mind if I put a bet on the favourite.'

Anna had a bright idea. 'Think hard, Grandpa. You were around in 1977. Can you remember which horse won the Grand National that year? Was it Wotagowa? If you could remember, we could be sure to bet on the winning horse.'

'It's no good,' Grandpa said after he'd had a quick think. 'My mind's suddenly gone blank. I haven't got the foggiest idea which horse won.'

The day before the Grand National, and Wotagowa is ready for the big race.

Ryan wasn't surprised. 'I bet it's Merlin who's blanked out your memory. He doesn't want us to tinker with history, remember.'

The loudspeakers crackled into life again. 'We have some bad news. Wotagowa, the favourite to win the Grand National, has been nobbled. He will not be able to run in the race.'

Ryan, Anna and Grandpa exchanged knowing glances. 'Well, there's one thing we *can* bet on,' said Grandpa, 'and that's another mystery to solve!'

The Mystery of the Nobbled Racehorse
Take a good look at the words and pictures and then decide who nobbled Wotagowa!

Everyone is sure he's going to win.

But that night . . .

Events of the year

Racehorse Red Rum wins the Grand National for the third time.

Britain celebrates the Queen's Silver Jubilee – 25 glorious years.

Star Wars and *Jaws* are huge hits at the cinema.

There are only three suspects: who did it?

Oliver Golightly   Steve Small   Lady Byrd

If you choose . . .	Secret Message letter	Next go to . . .
Lady Byrd	O	1954
Steve Small	R	1960
Oliver Golightly	E	1986

1978

'Babies everywhere!' Wherever they looked, there were babies. Babies crawling on the floor or lying on their backs with their legs in the air. Babies playing with furry animals and hitting each other on the head with rattles. And babies crying and screaming.

'What a terrible noise,' complained Anna, but Ryan didn't seem to mind. He picked up one of the crying babies and rocked it in his arms until it started gurgling and blowing bubbles.

'You've got the knack all right,' smiled Grandpa.

Ryan put the baby down again. 'It's how I stop my little sister crying,' he explained. Anna had, meanwhile, been looking for clues.

She returned with some news. 'This is a bouncing baby contest,' she told the others. 'They're all here to have their photos taken. And look at this leaflet I found. One of the babies was trying to eat it!'

They opened the chewed leaflet and inside found this . . .

The Bouncing Baby Challenge
Here are twelve beautiful, bouncing babies. Which one is the odd one out?

If you choose . . .	Secret Message letter	Next go to . . .
A baby from numbers 1–4	E	1955
A baby from numbers 5–8	A	1945
A baby from numbers 9–12	I	1985

Events of the year

The first test-tube baby, Louise Brown, is born.

Daley Thompson wins the Commonwealth gold medal in the decathlon – his first major title.

Superman is the big movie of the year.

The first non-Italian Pope for 400 years is elected. He comes from Poland and is known as Pope John Paul II.

1979

Before they knew what had happened, the three time-travellers found themselves sitting on a bench in the middle of a leafy park. Near by was a pond and some ducks came up quacking loudly.

'Poor things,' said Anna. 'We haven't got any bread to feed them.'

Their attention was distracted from the ducks, however, by a loud rustling from a nearby bush. A tall person in a broad-brimmed hat and a long raincoat edged out from the foliage and came and sat on the bench.

'I'm MI5 agent 487360,' he said, glancing around as if he was afraid someone might see him. 'Mr X sent me from HQ with an SOS for you.'

'Mr X, eh? Otherwise known as Merlin, I bet,' nodded Grandpa knowingly.

Computer genius.
Extremely clever.
Always carries a gun.
Very dangerous.

Mistress of disguise.
Always wears high heels.
More clever than she looks.
Goes to the theatre a lot.

The muscles of the gang.
Likes working out.
Has a bald spot at back of head.
Greedy and nasty.

Agent 487360 drew a folder from under his coat. 'We're trying to track down the members of the Klang Gang, a notorious group of criminals who are currently in Britain. We've staked them out and taken pictures of them, but we can't be certain we have the right people. Can you help?'

'We'll give it a go,' said Ryan cheerfully. 'We're getting quite good at puzzles!' So agent 487360 handed them the folder and, with a glance all round, melted back into the foliage. Anna opened the folder and they spread the contents on the grass. This is what they found.

The Klang Gang Challenge
In one of these pictures all three members of the Klang Gang have been caught together. Use the information to work out which picture it is.

Events of the year

Sir Anthony Blunt, art expert to the Queen, is revealed to have been a Russian agent.

Margaret Thatcher becomes the first woman Prime Minister of Britain.

If you choose . . .	Secret Message letter	Next go to . . .
1	R	1982
2 or 4	M	1964
5 or 6	F	1946

1980

'Hey, we're at the zoo!' cried Ryan. 'Let's go and see the elephants.' He dashed off through the crowd with Anna and Grandpa hard on his heels. They watched as the elephants were hosed down and scrubbed with a scratchy broom by the keeper.

'Where shall we go next?' asked Anna. 'I want to see the lions and tigers or the penguins.'

Grandpa was fiddling around with something in his pocket. 'What's this?' he said, as he pulled a guidebook out. 'Where did *that* come from?'

'I can guess,' laughed Ryan. 'It must be a present from Merlin.' The centre pages showed a map of the zoo. *Begin your trail around the zoo with a visit to the elephants*, it read. *Next, go to see the pandas*.

'Come on,' said Grandpa, 'you can see what it says. Off to the pandas.' And when they got to the panda enclosure, they found this pinned on the fence:

The Zoo Challenge
Here is a list of sixteen animals you can see in the zoo. Fifteen of them will fit into this word grid. Which one is left out?

Hippopotamus	Gorilla	Llama
Rattlesnake	Giraffe	Bison
Chimpanzee	Ostrich	Lemur
Crocodile	Cheetah	Hyena
Penguin	Lizard	Lion
Vulture		

Events of the year

The first panda is born in captivity.

Ex-actor Ronald Reagan is elected President of the USA.

If you choose . . .	Secret Message letter	Next go to . . .
Gorilla	O	1977
Vulture	E	1944
Bison	A	1960

1981

The next thing they knew, they were standing at the back of a small church. The other pews were crowded with people all dressed up for a wedding, and at the altar stood a bride and groom. They'd obviously arrived near the end of the service, for it was soon over and the family gathered outside the church for photographs.

'Hey, look what I've found,' said Ryan, feeling in his pockets, and he pulled out handfuls of confetti, which he and Anna threw at the bride. Grandpa was more interested in the old Rolls-Royce that was waiting.

'I wouldn't mind one of these myself,' he said, stroking the gleaming paintwork.

'Where's everyone off to now?' asked Ryan, when everyone began to leave. 'Are they going home?'

'Don't be silly,' Anna said. 'I went to a wedding when one of Mum's friends got married. After the church service, we all went to a hotel for lunch. We had strawberries and wedding cake and there was a disco. It was great.'

Events of the year

Prince Charles and Lady Diana Spencer are married in St Paul's Cathedral.

In France the use of the guillotine to behead criminals is, at last, abolished.

'Can't we go and have some lunch too?' Ryan wanted to know.

Grandpa shook his head. 'I don't think we've been invited to the wedding breakfast. But never mind, Ryan – I've found something else that might interest you.' And he held out an envelope containing six photos and a note which said:

The Wedding Day Challenge
These photos were taken on Brian and Bertha Backstop's wedding day. Unfortunately, they've got muddled up. Which order should they be in?

If you choose . . .	Secret Message letter	Next go to . . .
4, 1, 3, 6, 5, 2	C	1978
5, 2, 6, 3, 1, 4	T	1966
3, 6, 1, 5, 2, 4	R	1948

1982

'What are they doing, Grandpa?' asked Anna. 'Are they fishing for something?'

'You don't use a crane for fishing!' Ryan raised his eyebrows in disgust. Grandpa just scratched his head. And then suddenly he realized what was going on.

'I remember. They're raising the wreck of the *Mary Rose*.'

'Who's Mary Rose?' both kids wanted to know.

'She was a ship, a long time ago – when King Henry VIII was on the throne.'

'Was he the one with eight wives?' Ryan asked.

'No,' corrected Anna, 'he only had *six* wives.'

'And he also had this ship,' Grandpa continued. 'She

The year is 1545 and the *Mary Rose* is preparing for battle.

was a warship, and she was sailing out of the harbour one day to go to battle against the French, when she suddenly sank. And now they've found what's left of her and they're raising her again. If you'd like to, we can go and see her in Portsmouth once we get back to the 1990s.'

Ryan was puzzled. 'Why did she sink?'

Grandpa shrugged. 'I don't think anyone really knows,' he replied. 'But I suppose we could try to find out . . .'

The Mystery of the *Mary Rose*
Take a good look at this story and see if you can work out why the Mary Rose capsized.

Security is tight . . .

118

There are only three suspects:
Dan Archer; Swashbuckling Cyril;
and Cannonmaster Pete.

Events of the year

The *Mary Rose* is brought to the surface.

Argentinian troops invade the Falkland Islands in the South Atlantic. British troops are sent to regain the islands. The war ends in British victory.

Who sank the *Mary Rose*?

If you choose . . .	Secret Message letter	Next go to . . .
Dan Archer	A	1943
Swashbuckling Cyril	O	1957
Cannonmaster Pete	E	1964

1983

Anna, Ryan and Grandpa clung nervously to the palm tree they were sitting in. Below them a large crocodile slid out of the water and came up the sand to the tree. It looked up hungrily and opened its jaws wide. 'Help!' murmured Grandpa. Ryan quickly grabbed a coconut from one of the branches and threw it down at the croc.

The coconut landed on the croc's head with a loud thump. The crocodile roared, looked a bit dazed, and dived back into the water.

'We've got a few minutes before that greedy-guts comes back,' said Ryan, 'but we're going to have to find a way off this island soon – otherwise our quest for the Golden Puffin will end here.'

'But there *is* no way off,' groaned Anna. 'The water's full of crocodiles.'

'And there are poisonous snakes everywhere too,' added Ryan.

Grandpa shook his head in disbelief. 'Merlin wouldn't have put us here if there wasn't some way out. All we have to do is find it.'

Events of the year

A ship sinks in the crocodile-infested River Nile and 500 people are reported killed – or eaten.

It becomes illegal to travel in the front of the car without wearing a seatbelt.

Breakfast television begins with the BBC's *Breakfast Time*.

The Desert Island Challenge
Can you work out a way of getting the three time-travellers to safety? Where will your route take them – to the boat, the jetty or the beach?

If you choose . . .	Secret Message letter	Next go to . . .
Boat	N	1965
Jetty	T	1991
Beach	L	1976

1984

Ryan sniffed suspiciously. 'Something's burning,' he said.

Anna pointed upwards. 'Look, there's smoke coming from over there – and flames too!'

The three of them ran through the darkening streets until they reached the source of the fire. It was a huge church, and it was blazing away.

'I know this place,' said Grandpa in surprise. 'It's York Minster. Me and your grandma came here for a day trip only a few years ago – or a few years in the future, maybe. It's all very confusing if you think too much about it.'

They stood and watched as people in their pyjamas ran in and out of the flaming minster, rescuing pictures and gold plates and all the treasure of the church. Just

then a fire-engine came screeching to a halt and firemen leapt out and began unrolling their hoses. Soon more and more firefighters arrived to put out the blaze.

Anna watched it all with a rather puzzled expression. Finally she said, 'I think my eyes must be going wrong. Either that, or there are some *very* funny things happening here tonight.'

'I'm glad you said that,' Grandpa admitted with relief. 'I thought *my* eyes were playing tricks too!'

The Firefighters' Challenge

If you look closely at this picture of the York Minster blaze, you'll see that there are some rather strange things going on. How many absurdities can you spot in the picture?

Events of the year

The best-selling record of the year is 'Do They Know It's Christmas?' by Band Aid, which raises millions of pounds to help fight the famine in Ethiopia.

Scientists report that British lakes and forests are being destroyed by acid rain.

If you spot . . .	Secret Message letter	Next go to . . .
4	B	1947
6	C	1963
10	D	1971

1985

This time the three of them were transported slap-bang on to a stage. A piano and a drum-kit were waiting to be played, and in front of the stage a huge crowd of people were waiting. 'It's a pop concert!' cried Anna. 'I hope it's Bros.'

'Nope,' said Ryan, looking at a banner hanging across the stage. 'It's Stevie Sparkle and the Purple Halibut Band. I've never heard of them, but they sound really bad.'

At that moment a couple of people came on stage and began to practise the drums and tune a guitar very

---

The Purple Halibut Murder Mystery

If you follow these clues, they should lead you to the murderer. There are four suspects. They are:
Terry Riff, lead guitarist of Purple Halibut;
Tanya Tonsils, backing singer with the band;
Howey Doowin, the band's drummer;
Coll Fillins, the keyboard player.

Clues:

1. The murderer entered Stevie's dressing-room through a door linking their two rooms.

2. Terry and Tanya had dressing-rooms that were exactly the same size.

3. Howey had the smallest dressing-room.

4. Stevie's dressing-room adjoined those of Howey, Coll and Terry.

5. Tanya didn't do it.

Who murdered Stevie Sparkle?

Events of the year

By organizing the Live Aid concerts in London and Philadelphia, Bob Geldof raises millions of pounds to help the starving in Ethiopia.

loudly. Grandpa winced. 'This isn't my cup of tea. I'd prefer some nice Val Doonican any day.'

His words were interrupted by a scream. 'Stevie Sparkle has been murdered in his dressing-room!' someone shouted. There was instant uproar.

'I wonder if this is a mystery for us to solve,' said Grandpa, glancing at a nearby table. 'Look, here's a plan of their dressing-rooms.'

'And I've found a list of clues,' added Anna. 'Maybe if we put the two together, we can work out who the murderer is.'

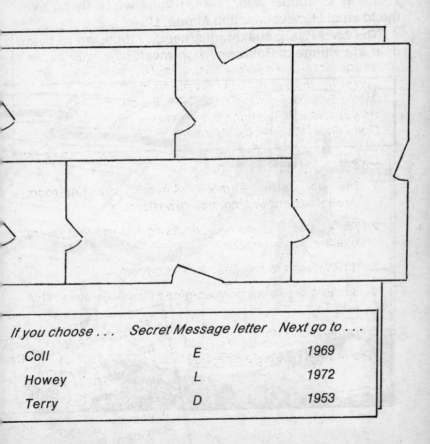

If you choose . . .	Secret Message letter	Next go to . . .
Coll	E	1969
Howey	L	1972
Terry	D	1953

1986

'This is the nicest form of flying I've ever tried,' said Grandpa approvingly, as they slid silently through the sky in the basket of a hot-air balloon. Anna leaned over the side to get a good look at the view. She could see part of the coastline and a small town.

'I'm trying to work out where we are,' responded Ryan, turning the pages of the map-book he'd found in the basket. 'It's a bit difficult to tell. There are at least three possible places.' He showed them the maps and they all studied them.

Finally Grandpa said, 'Well, I think we're flying over the town of Hunkybunsett in Maine, USA.'

'No,' said Ryan, shaking his head, '*I* think we're flying over the village of Poltroon in Cornwall.'

'You're both wrong,' said Anna. 'It's plain to me that we're flying over Sudfin-sur-Mer in the South of France.'

'Well, we'd better get it right,' commented Grandpa, 'or otherwise we could drift out to sea and be totally lost!'

The Balloon Challenge
Look at the three maps and decide for yourself who's right – Anna, Ryan or Grandpa.

If you choose . . .	Secret Message letter	Next go to . . .
Sudfin-sur-Mer	D	1942
Hunkybunsett	S	1973
Poltroon	B	1954

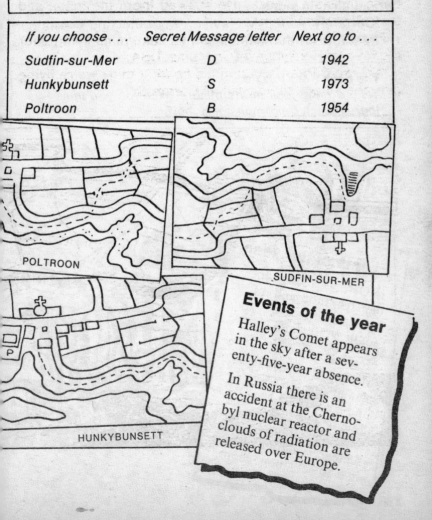

POLTROON

SUDFIN-SUR-MER

Events of the year

Halley's Comet appears in the sky after a seventy-five-year absence.

In Russia there is an accident at the Chernobyl nuclear reactor and clouds of radiation are released over Europe.

HUNKYBUNSETT

1987

Deep in the muddy waters of Loch Ness, Grandpa, Anna and Ryan were chugging along in a small submarine captained by Professor Magnus McTavish.

Professor McTavish twiddled the dials of his sonar machine and switched on the radar. 'Och, look at this,' he said. 'Not even a wee blip or bleep!'

Grandpa was thoughtful. 'You believe that if there *was* a monster living in this loch, your sonar and radar would pick up signs of it?'

'Certainly,' cried McTavish. 'My detecting equipment is infallible. With these machines I can pinpoint a needle

The Loch Ness Puzzle
Take a good look at the picture. What do you think – is there a Loch Ness monster or not?

Events of the year

In October a hurricane damages thousands of homes and trees in southern England.

Nineteen-year-old Mathias Rust flies a small plane to Moscow and lands in Red Square. For this amazing feat he is sentenced to four years in a Soviet labour camp.

in a haystack. I'm telling you a scientific fact – there *is* no Loch Ness monster. It doesn't exist.'

'Excuse me,' cried Ryan, tugging at the Professor's sleeve.

'Yes, child?' said McTavish.

'I saw a monster behind that rock over there.'

'Nonsense, there's no such thing as a monster – didn't you hear me just say so?' snapped the Professor. Ryan was quiet.

'I saw something too,' said Anna, 'but I think it was just a log swaying in the weed.'

'Well, I can't see anything,' said Grandpa, peering out. 'You two are starting to imagine things!' Or are they?

If you choose . . .	Secret Message letter	Next go to . . .
Yes	F	1970
No	N	1958
Don't know	B	1962

1988

Grandpa, Anna and Ryan stood at the top of the ski-jump and looked down it. The ground sloped so steeply away from them that they all felt a bit giddy. 'You wouldn't catch *me* hurling myself down there,' said Grandpa.

At that moment a ski-jumper came whooshing down the jump at tremendous speed and went flying off the end. He hung in the air for what seemed like ages, before landing gracefully almost 100 metres away. The loudspeakers announced the length of his jump.

'Jean-Paul Sillie of France has jumped 99.6 metres. The next to jump will be Sid the Sparrow of Britain.' With a blood-curdling yell, Sid went tearing off down the jump, took off, did a somersault and landed in a pile of snow. 'Sid the Sparrow jumped 11.7 metres,' it was announced.

'Whoops!' laughed Ryan and Grandpa. A little while later, they saw Sid climbing back up the slope towards them. He waved at them.

'That last jump was terrible,' he admitted. 'I've managed to go much further than that.'

Events of the year

Gold-medal-winning athlete Ben Johnson of Canada is disgraced after it's revealed that he took drugs to help him run faster.

Edwina Currie says that most eggs are infected with salmonella. Egg sales fall dramatically.

Eddie the Eagle comes last in the ski-jumping at the Winter Olympics.

'How far exactly?' asked Ryan.

Sid handed them a big brown envelope. 'Well, my old friend Merlin told me that it's up to *you* to work that out.' And with that he was off to have another attempt.

The Ski-Jump Challenge
In the envelope was this picture. As you can see, part of it has been torn. If you assemble the correct bits, you will be able to see how long Sid's best jump was.

If you choose ...	Secret Message letter	Next go to ...
30 metres	A	1974
40 metres	O	1950
65 metres	E	1949

1989

'Hey, that's the Eiffel Tower – so now we've come to Paris!' exclaimed Anna, pointing to the famous landmark.

'I've got a joke about Paris,' announced Ryan. 'What happened to the man who took twenty tins of prunes on holiday to Paris?'

'I don't know,' said Grandpa.

'He spent all the time in the Louvre!' cried Ryan, shrieking with laughter. When they'd recovered, Grandpa spotted a poster advertising an exhibition.

'This sounds interesting,' he said. 'It's an exhibition about the French Revolution, which happened 200 years ago this year.'

The Mystery of the Missing Jewels
Take a look at this story. Can you work out who stole the necklace?

Today Revolutionary Exhibition Opens . . .

'I wouldn't mind seeing the guillotine they used to chop people's heads off,' said Ryan, who was in a bloodthirsty mood.

Anna was reading about the other exhibits. 'I'd like to see Queen Marie Antoinette's priceless diamonds,' she decided. So off the three of them went. But when they got to the museum, they found the doors barred by a *gendarme*.

'You cannot come een,' he told them. 'Ze diamond necklace zat belonged to Marie Antoinette 'as bin stolen. We are looking for ze thief.'

Grandpa turned to the children and said, 'It sounds as if it's the kind of mystery we might be able to solve.'

The exhibits include a guillotine and Queen Marie Antoinette's priceless diamonds!

Events of the year

The Berlin Wall is torn down.

In China students are massacred by troops after staging demonstrations for democracy.

In Russia a seven-year-old boy grew to a height of six foot and weighed fourteen stone.

Many people come to look . . .

> and one person has come to steal!!!

If you choose ...	Secret Message letter	Next go to ...
Monsieur Neli	I	1975
Monsieur Belli	U	1967
Mademoiselle Jeli	A	1956

The police have searched the pockets of the three suspects but found nothing. Which one of them stole the diamonds?

MADEMOISELLE JELI   MONSIEUR BELLI   MONSIEUR NELI

1990

Grandpa, Anna and Ryan raised their candles and inspected the cold, slimy stone walls of the place they found themselves in. 'At a guess,' Grandpa said, 'I'd say we were in a castle dungeon.'

'Well, let's get out,' said Anna firmly. 'Look, there's a trap-door up there.' She and Grandpa were just about to walk into the darkness beyond when Ryan called out.

'Stop! I've found something else,' he cried. Carved deep into the wall was a message. *Only one person may pass through each gate*, it read. *If two or three shall try, then all will fail*.

'That was a close shave!' breathed Grandpa. 'We might have been stuck here for ever.' His eyes fell on some steps that led even deeper beneath the castle. 'Here's another way out – though it doesn't look very nice down there.'

'And look at this,' called Ryan. He'd found an old iron ladder that went up through a hole in the ceiling of the dungeon.

'Well, there's nothing for it,' said Grandpa. 'We'll each have to try a separate way out. I'll volunteer to go down the steps.'

'And I'll go up this ladder,' said Ryan.

'Which leaves me with the trap-door,' said Anna. 'Good luck!' And off all three went.

Events of the year

Nelson Mandela is freed from prison after more than twenty years.

The Queen Mother is ninety years old.

East and West Germany decide to join together to become one country.

England reaches the semi-finals of the World Cup!

The Dungeon Challenge

Which of the three time-travellers has the shortest journey out of the castle?

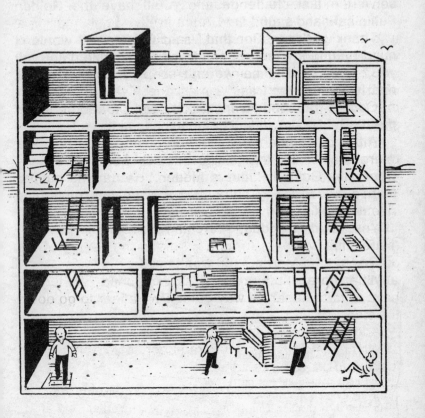

If you choose . . .	Secret Message letter	Next go to . . .
Grandpa	R	1961
Ryan	D	1946
Anna	M	1979

1991

'Congratulations!' cried Merlin when the three time-travellers at last arrived back in the present day. 'You've done the most difficult bit. Now all you have to do is solve the last challenge and you'll have the Golden Puffin safe and sound.'

'Thank goodness for that,' said Grandpa. 'I wouldn't mind putting my feet up and having a snooze, I can tell you.' Ryan and Anna weren't so pleased that they'd nearly finished the trail.

'Ooooh,' moaned Ryan, 'I don't want to stop yet. It's great!' But Merlin wasn't going to change the rules.

'All good things have to come to an end,' he said. 'Here are all the things you need to work out exactly where the Golden Puffin is hidden.' He handed them a map, a guidebook and a postcard. 'Have you still got the rhyme I sent you?' he asked Grandpa.

'Yes,' said Grandpa, searching through his pockets. 'Here it is.'

'Good,' said Merlin. 'You won't need anything else.'

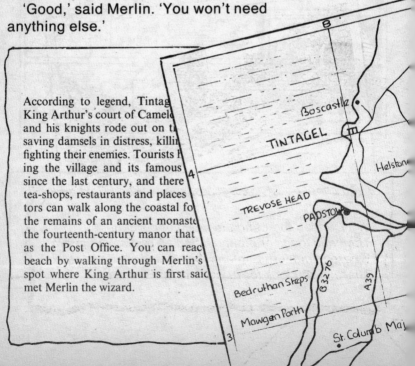

According to legend, Tintag
King Arthur's court of Camel
and his knights rode out on t
saving damsels in distress, killi
fighting their enemies. Tourists
ing the village and its famous
since the last century, and there
tea-shops, restaurants and places
tors can walk along the coastal fo
the remains of an ancient monaste
the fourteenth-century manor that
as the Post Office. You can reac
beach by walking through Merlin's
spot where King Arthur is first said
met Merlin the wizard.

The Golden Puffin Challenge

This is the final challenge. You can use the rhyme, the guidebook, the postcard and the map to work out the name of the building – not just the place or the map reference – where the Golden Puffin is hidden. And there's something else that will help you. Turn to the back page of this book, where you've written all the letters you've collected as you've gone along. If you've got all fifty puzzles right, you'll find a very useful clue.

When you have worked out the answer, write it in the space provided on the final page. Fill in your name and address, then cut the page very carefully out of the book and send it to: Search for the Golden Puffin, PUFFIN BOOKS, 27 Wrights Lane, London W8 5TZ by 19 December, 1991. If you've got the answer right, you will be entered in the Golden Puffin draw – and you could win the Golden Puffin!

In a Cornish river find the beast of burden,
Then add loads or plenty to find an ancient kingdom,
Where in modern England this ruined castle lies,
There, if you look for it, you will find the prize.

THE COMPETITION

Every time you answer a puzzle, you'll get a letter. Enter it here, in the box next to the correct year. By the time you get to 1991, you may find that you have a useful clue to help you solve the search for the Golden Puffin!

1st Attempt

1941 ☐	1950 ☐	1959 ☐	1968 ☐	1977 ☐	1986 ☐
1942 ☐	1951 ☐	1960 ☐	1969 ☐	1978 ☐	1987 ☐
1943 ☐	1952 ☐	1961 ☐	1970 ☐	1979 ☐	1988 ☐
1944 ☐	1953 ☐	1962 ☐	1971 ☐	1980 ☐	1989 ☐
1945 ☐	1954 ☐	1963 ☐	1972 ☐	1981 ☐	1990 ☐
1946 ☐	1955 ☐	1964 ☐	1973 ☐	1982 ☐	1991 ☐
1947 ☐	1956 ☐	1965 ☐	1974 ☐	1983 ☐	
1948 ☐	1957 ☐	1966 ☐	1975 ☐	1984 ☐	
1949 ☐	1958 ☐	1967 ☐	1976 ☐	1985 ☐	

2nd Attempt

1941 ☐	1950 ☐	1959 ☐	1968 ☐	1977 ☐	1986 ☐
1942 ☐	1951 ☐	1960 ☐	1969 ☐	1978 ☐	1987 ☐
1943 ☐	1952 ☐	1961 ☐	1970 ☐	1979 ☐	1988 ☐
1944 ☐	1953 ☐	1962 ☐	1971 ☐	1980 ☐	1989 ☐
1945 ☐	1954 ☐	1963 ☐	1972 ☐	1981 ☐	1990 ☐
1946 ☐	1955 ☐	1964 ☐	1973 ☐	1982 ☐	1991 ☐
1947 ☐	1956 ☐	1965 ☐	1974 ☐	1983 ☐	
1948 ☐	1957 ☐	1966 ☐	1975 ☐	1984 ☐	
1949 ☐	1958 ☐	1967 ☐	1976 ☐	1985 ☐	

When you have worked out where the Golden Puffin is hidden, write the answer in the space below. Then fill in your name, address, telephone number and age, tear this page carefully out of the book and send it to:

SEARCH FOR THE GOLDEN PUFFIN
PUFFIN BOOKS
27 Wrights Lane
London W8 5TZ

by 19 December 1991.
If your answer is correct, it will be entered in a draw and the winner will receive a Golden Puffin.

The draw will take place on 20 December 1991.

The winner will be notified by post by 29 December 1991.

The Golden Puffin is hidden at:

....

My name is: ....

My address is: ....

....

....

My telephone number is: ....

I am .... *years old*